100 ANCIENT CHINESE MINIATURE STORIES

中國歷代極短篇一百則

一百叢書⑯

漢英對照 Chinese-English

馬家駒編譯

100

ANCIENT CHINESE

MINIATURE

STORIES

中國歷代
極短篇一百則

臺灣商務印書館發行

《一百叢書》總序

　　本館出版英漢（或漢英）對照《一百叢書》的目的，是希望憑藉着英、漢兩種語言的對譯，把中國和世界各類著名作品的精華部分介紹給中外讀者。

　　本叢書的涉及面很廣。題材包括了寓言、詩歌、散文、短篇小說、書信、演說、語錄、神話故事、聖經故事、成語故事、名著選段等等。

　　顧名思義，《一百叢書》中的每一種都由一百個單元組成。以一百為單位，主要是讓編譯者在浩瀚的名著中作挑選時有一個取捨的最低和最高限額。至於取捨的標準，則是見仁見智，各有心得。

　　由於各種書中被選用的篇章節段，都是以原文或已被認定的範本作藍本，而譯文又經專家學者們精雕細琢，千錘百煉，故本叢書除可作為各種題材的精選讀本外，也是研習英漢兩種語言對譯的理想參考書，部分更可用作朗誦教材。外國學者如要研習漢語，本叢書亦不失為理想工具。

商務印書館（香港）有限公司
編輯部

前　言

　　商務印書館請我編譯一本《中國歷代極短篇一百則》。在中國古代，並沒有極短篇這個名詞，也很難找到它的確切的同義詞。不過從春秋末期到鴉片戰爭爆發的二千多年間，積存下來大量的古典著作，特別是所謂筆記小說裏卻有無數字數不多而含義深刻雋永的短文章，性質相當於英國文學裏的特寫、軼事、隨筆、小品之類，反映了古代中國人民的智慧、幽默、為人處世的態度和社會生活。

　　本書起自先秦，下迄清代，選擇了各個時期具有一定代表性和一定情節的短篇作品--百則。限於篇幅，難免使讀者有"淺嘗即止"的感覺，但如果能夠從中略為了解到中國古代文化的吉光片羽，也就不是白費工夫了。

　　因為文化背景不同，語言結構懸殊，漢譯英和英譯漢一樣，都會遇到一些難以完全達意的地方。關於這一點，凡是翻譯工作者都有同感，這裏就不再多說了。本來想多作一些注釋，但有些問題不是一條注釋或幾句話所能說得清楚，因此覺得除極少數情況外，不如留給好學深思、願意進一步研究的讀者自己去解決為是。

參加翻譯工作的有尚端、江載芬兩女士和鄒孝標先生（以所譯篇數多寡為序），特此表示衷心的感謝。

馬家駒（里千）
一九九三年十二月二十四日

FOREWORD

The Commercial Press asked me to translate and edit 100 ancient Chinese miniature stories. Although the expression "miniature story" does not occur in ancient Chinese writings, it is hard to find a more appropriate synonym, and we have no difficulty in finding a great number of short articles in classical works, especially in the historical annals from the late Spring and Autumn Period (770-467 B.C.) to the outbreak of the Opium War in 1840.

These articles, some of which consist of merely a few words, are comparable to English features, anecdotes, comments, jottings or short essays. They display both wit and humour, as well as the various attitudes towards life and the general aspects of the ancient Chinese society.

We have selected 100 representative and interesting pieces from the Pre-Qin Period right through to the Qing Dynasty, covering more than two thousand five hundred years. Due to the shortness of this compilation, readers may feel that they can only catch a glimpse of Chinese culture, yet it should be sufficient to gain an insight into this subject.

Because of the difference in cultural background and the disparity of linguistic constructs, Chinese-English translation fails to convey the original idea perfectly, just as with English-Chinese translation. I think all translators agree with me on this. We could have given more annotations, however some problems cannot be explained by an annotation of only a few words. Therefore in many cases, we have decided to leave such problems to the interested readers themselves to study and research into.

I am greatly indebted personally to Shang Duan, Jiang Zaifen and Zhou Xiaobiao for their contributions to the translations in this book (names arranged in sequence of number of articles translated).

Ma Jiaju (Liqian)
Dec. 24, 1993

目錄

1. 孔門弟子

　　子路、曾晳、冉有、公西華[1] 侍坐。子曰：“以吾一日長乎爾，毋吾以也。居則曰：‘不吾知也，’如或知爾，則何以哉？”子路率爾而對曰：“千乘之國，攝乎大國之間，加之以師旅，因之以饑饉，由也為之，比及三年，可使有勇，且知方也。”夫子哂之。“求，爾何如？”對曰：“方六七十，如五六十，求也為之，比及三年，可使足民，如其禮樂，以俟君子。”“赤，爾何如？”對曰：“非曰能之，願學焉。宗廟之事，如會同，端章甫，願為小相焉。”“點，爾何如？”鼓瑟希，鏗爾。舍瑟而作。對曰：“異乎三子者之撰。”子

---

(1) 仲由，字子路；曾點，字晳；冉求，字有；公西赤，字華，都是孔子的學生。

1. Confucius and His Pupils

Zilu (Zhong You), Zeng Xi (Dian), Ran You (Qiu) and Gongxi Hua (Chi) were sitting beside Confucius (551-476 BC). Confucius said to them, "Don't mind my being slightly older than you, just answer me directly. You always say, 'The ruler does not know me.' If you were known to some ruler, what would you like to do?"

Zilu hastily replied, "In the case of a state of a thousand chariots confined between other large states, suffering from invasions and stricken with famine, if I were appointed to the government, in less than three years' time I could make the people brave and recognize the right conduct." The Master smiled.

"Qiu, what are your wishes?"

Ran You replied, "Suppose there was a state of sixty or seventy square $li^{(1)}$, or one of fifty or sixty, and I was entrusted with the government of it, in three years I could make the people wealthy. As to teaching them the rites and music, I would leave that job to other more able men."

"Chi, What are your wishes?" said the Master to Gongxi Hua.

"I do not say I am able, but I should wish to learn. In the services of the ancestral temple, and at the conferences of the princes, I would like to be a small assistant, wearing a black robe and a cap of ceremony," Kongxi Hua replied.

Last of all the Master asked Zeng Xi, "Dian, what are your wishes?"

Xi, stopped playing his $se^{(2)}$, laid the instrument aside, rose and said, "My wishes are different from my three friends'."

---

(1) 1 *li* = 0.5 km
(2) *se*: a twenty-five-stringed plucked instrument somewhat similar to the zither.

曰：“何傷乎，亦各言其志也。”曰：“莫春者，春服既成，冠者五六人，童子六七人，浴乎沂，風乎舞雩，詠而歸。”夫子喟然歎曰：“吾與點也。”

三子者出，曾皙後。曾皙曰：“夫三子者之言何如？”子曰：“亦各言其志也已矣。”曰：“夫子何哂由也？”曰：“為國以禮，其言不讓，是故哂之。”“唯求則非邦也與？”“安見方六七十如五六十，而非邦也者？”“唯赤則非邦也與？”“宗廟會同，非諸侯而何？赤也為之小，孰能為之大？”

《論語·先進》

"Never mind," said the Master. "Just speak out your wishes all the same."

"In the last month of spring, dressed up for the season and accompanied by five or six young men over twenty and six or seven young boys, I would bathe in the Yi River, enjoy the gentle breeze over the rain altar and then sing on the way home."

The Master sighed, "I appreciate Dian."

After the three others had left, Zeng Xi said to the Master, "What do you think of the words of my three friends?"

"Each of them simply expressed his wishes," replied the Master.

Xi pursued: "Master, why did you smile at You?"

"The management of a state demands the rites and rules of courtesy. His words were not modest, so I smiled at him," the Master replied.

Xi again said, "But was it not a state which Qiu proposed for himself?"

"Yes, did you ever see a territory of sixty or seventy square li, or one of fifty or sixty, which was not a state?"

"And was it not a state which Chi proposed for himself?"

The Master replied again, "Yes, who but dukes and princes has the privilege to deal with ancestral temples and be present at court? If Chi were to be a small assistant in those services, who could be a great one?"

Lunyu (The Analects of Confucius)

2. 不知天寒

　　景公之時，雨雪三日而不霽。公被狐白之裘，坐於堂側陛。晏子[1]入見，立有間，公曰：“怪哉！雨雪三日而天不寒。”晏子對曰：“天不寒乎？”公笑。晏子曰：“嬰聞古之賢君，飽而知人之飢，溫而知人之寒，逸而知人之勞。今君不知也。”

《晏子春秋·內篇》

---

(1) 晏子：晏嬰，齊景公的宰相。

2. Feeling No Cold

Once during the reign of King Jing (?-490 BC) in the State of Qi[(1)], it had been snowing for three days without break.

The King, dressed in a white fox fur cape, was sitting in a porch on one side of the palace . The Prime Minister Yan Zi (?-500 BC) came to present himself to the King. After he stood before the King for a while, the King spoke to him, "Strange, it has been snowing for three days without break, but still I don't feel cold."

At this Yan Zi asked of the King, "Is it actually not cold?"

The King just smiled. Yan Zi spoke out again, "I have heard that the ancient kings of virtue knew that the people were hungry while they themselves were full, that the people were cold while they were warm and that the people were exhausted by hard work while they were in comfort and at leisure. How could Your Majesty know nothing of all these?"

Yan Zi Chun Qiu (Anecdotes of Yan Ying)

---

(1) Qi: a state in the Spring and Autumn Period (770-476 BC) in Chinese history.

3. 齊人有一妻一妾者

　　齊人有一妻一妾而處室者，其良人出，則必饜酒肉
而後返。其妻問所與飲食者，則盡富貴也。其妻告其妾
曰："良人出則必饜酒肉而後返。問其與飲食者，盡富
貴也，而未嘗有顯者來。吾將瞷良人之所之也。"
蚤（早）起，施從良人之所之。徧國中無與立談者。卒
之東郭墦間之祭者，乞其餘不足，又顧而之他，此其為
饜足之道也。其妻歸，告其妾，曰："良人者，所仰望
而終身也，今若此。"與其妾訕其良人，而相泣於中
庭。而良人未之知也，施施從外來，驕其妻妾。由君子
觀之，則人之所以求富貴利達者，其妻妾不羞也，而不
相泣者幾希矣。

《孟子・離婁下》

8

3. A Shameless Fellow

A man of the State of Qi had a wife and a concubine living with him together. Whenever the husband went out, he would get himself well filled with wine and meat before he returned. His wife asked him whom he ate and drank with, he said that all of them were wealthy and honorable people. The wife then said to the concubine, "Whenever our husband goes out, he is sure to come back having satiated with wine and meat. I asked with whom he ate and drank, and he said they were all wealthy and honourable people. And yet no people of distinction have ever come here. I will spy out where our husband has been to."

One day, she got up early in the morning, and followed her husband in secret to wherever he went. All along in the whole city, no one stopped to talk with him. At last, he came to those who were offering sacrifices among the tombs beyond the eastern outer wall, and begged for what they had left over. Not having had enough, he looked about for other leftovers. And this was the way in which he satisfied himself.

His wife returned, and informed the concubine, saying, "It is our husband that we look up to and rely on all our lives. But now these are his ways!" The wife and the concubine mocked at their husband and wept together in the middle room. Meanwhile the husband, knowing nothing of this, came in jauntily, appearing smugly in front of his wife and concubine.

From this, decent and upright people will see that few people can employ means of gaining wealth, honour and advancement which would not cause their wives and concubines to weep together in shame.

Meng Zi (The Works of Mencius)

4. 不龜手之藥

　　惠子謂莊子曰："魏王貽我大瓠之種，我樹之成而實五石，以盛水漿，其堅不能自舉也。剖之以為瓢，則瓠落無所容。非不呺然大也，吾為其無用而掊之。"

　　莊子曰："夫子固拙於用大矣。宋人有善為不龜（jūn）手之藥者，世世以洴澼絖為事。客聞之，請買其方百金。聚族而謀曰：'我世世為洴澼絖，不過數金；今一朝而鬻之百金，請與之。'客得之，以說吳王。越有難，吳王使之將，冬與越人水戰，大敗越人，裂地而封之。能不龜手，一也；或以封，或不免於洴澼

4. The Salve

Huizi told Zhuangzi (369-? BC): "The King of Wei[1] gave me some seeds of a large calabash. I sowed them, and the fruit, when fully grown, weighed five *dan*[2]. I used it to contain water, but it was too fragile to lift. I cut it in two and made two drinking vessels, but they were too flat to hold water. Nothing but large stuff! So I knocked them into pieces."

Zhuangzi said: "Sir, you're not wise in the use of the large calabash. A man of Song[3] was so skilful at making a salve, which kept the hands from getting chapped, that his family could for generations make the bleaching of ramee their business, even in winter. A stranger heard of this and intended to buy the recipe of the salve for a hundred *jin*[4] of gold. All the members of the clan gathered together and considered the offer: 'We've been bleaching ramee for generations and have earned only a little money. Now we can sell our recipe for a hundred *jin* overnight. Let the stranger have it!'"

"The stranger got it and took it to the King of the State of Wu[3] who was hostile to the State of Yue[3]. There he was placed in command of the fleet. With the recipe he was able to engage Yue in a battle in winter. He won a great victory, and was conferred a portion of the territory taken from Yue."

" In both cases the salve was employed to preserve the hands from being chapped. However in the latter case, it led to the land

---

(1) Wei: a state in the Warring States Period (475-221 3C) in Chinese history.
(2) 1 *dan* = 75 kg
(3) Song, Wu, Yue : three states in the Spring and Autumn Period (770-476 BC) in Chinese history.
(4) *jin*: an ancient monetary unit. 1 *jin* = 50 kgs. of gold

絖，則所用之異也。今子有五石之瓠，何不慮以為大樽而浮乎江湖，而憂其瓠落無所容？則夫子猶有蓬之心也夫！"

《莊子·逍遙游》

conferment; but in the former case, it had only enabled its owners to continue their bleaching business. The difference of results arises from the different applications of the recipe. Now you, sir, have huge calabashes of five *dan*. Why don't you think of making large vessels of them, by means of which you could have floated over rivers or lakes, instead of sorrowing over the discovery that they are useless for holding water? Your mind must have been confused."

Zhuang Zi (The Writings of Zhuang Zhou)

5. 開七竅

　　南海之帝為儵，北海之帝為忽，中央之帝為渾沌。儵與忽時相與遇於渾沌之地，渾沌待之甚善。儵與忽謀報渾沌之德，曰：“人皆有七竅以視聽食息，此獨無有，嘗試鑿之。”日鑿一竅，七日而渾沌死。

《莊子・應帝王》

5. Seven Orifices

The Emperor of the South Sea was Shu (Sudden), the Emperor of the North Sea was Hu (Swiftness), and the Emperor of the Centre was Hundun (Chaos). Shu and Hu often met on the land of Hundun, who was quite kind to them. They would like to repay his kindness, and said, "Men all have seven orifices — eyes, ears, mouth and nostrils for the purpose of seeing, hearing, eating and breathing, while this Emperor has none. Let's try and make them for him." Then they dug one orifice in Hundun every day, and on the seventh day Hundun died.

Zhuang Zi (The Writings of Zhuang Zhou)

6. 庖丁解牛

　　庖丁為文惠君解牛，手之所觸，肩之所倚，足之所履，膝之所踦，砉（xū）然嚮然，奏刀騞（huō）然，莫不中音。合於桑林[1]之舞，乃中經首[2]之會[3]。

　　文惠君曰：“譆，善哉！技蓋至此乎？”

　　庖丁釋刀對曰：“臣之所好者道也，進乎技矣。始臣之解牛之時，所見無非‘全’牛者。三年之後，未嘗見全牛也。方今之時，臣以神遇而不以目視，官知止而神欲行。依乎天理，批大郤，導大窾（kuǎn），因其固然。技經肯綮之未嘗，而況大軱乎！良庖歲更刀，割也；族庖月更刀，折也。今臣之刀十九年矣，所解數千牛矣，而刀刃若新發於硎。彼節者有閒，而刀刃者無

---

(1) 桑林：商代的一種舞蹈。
(2) 經首：堯時的樂曲。
(3) 會：合符節拍。

6. Cutting Up an Ox

The cook of King Wenhui was cutting up an ox for the king. Whenever he applied his hand, with his shoulders leaning forward, his foot firmly planted on the ground, and his knees exerting a pressure, in the audible ripping of the hide and the slicing operation of the knife, the sounds were all of a regular cadence. And both movement and sound proceeded as in the *sanglin* dance[1] and the *jingshou* music[2].

The King marvelled: "Oh, excellent! Your art is just perfect!"

The cook laid down his knife, and replied to the remark, "What I, your servant, follow are the principles of Tao, with which I can master this skill. When I first began to cut up an ox, I saw nothing more than the entire carcass. After three years I no longer saw it as a whole. Now I rely on my mental faculties instead of my eyesight. The use of my senses is discarded, while my mind takes me along. Following the natural lines, my knife slips through the great crevices and slices through the great cavities, and my art allows me to avoid the big bones.

"A good cook changes his knife every year and he cuts with it; an ordinary cook changes his every month and he chops with it. Now my knife has been in use for nineteen years and it has cut up several thousand oxen, and yet its edge is as sharp as if it had newly come from the whetstone. There are tendons in the joints, and the edge of the knife which is of little thickness can easily

---

(1) *sanglin* dance: a dance of the Shang Dynasty (c.16 thC -11thC BC).
(2) *jingshou* music: the music of ancient China in legendary history before the 21st century BC.

厚；以無厚入有間，恢恢乎其於遊刃必有餘地矣，是以十九年而刀刃若新發於硎。雖然，每至於族，吾見其難為，怵然為戒，視為止，行為遲。動刀甚微，謋然已解，如土委地。提刀而立，為之四顧，為之躊躇滿志，善刀而藏之。"

文惠君曰："善哉！吾聞庖丁之言，得養生焉。"

《莊子‧養生主》

slice in the tendons, and move along as if there were nothing there! That is the reason why my knife looks as if it had newly come from the whetstone after 19 years.

"Nevertheless, whenever I come to a complicated joint and see that there will be some difficulty, I will proceed anxiously and with caution, not allowing my eyes to wander away from the place, and moving my hand slowly. Then by a very slight movement, the part is quickly separated and drops like a clot of earth to the ground. Then standing with the knife in my hand, I will look about with great satisfaction, wipe the knife clean and put it in its sheath."

King Wenhui said, "Incredible! I have heard the words of my cook, and got from them the nourishment of life!"

Zhuang Zi (The Writings of Zhuang Zhou)

7. 小兒辯日

孔子東游，見兩小兒辯鬭。問其故。一兒曰："我以日始出時去人近，而日中時遠也。"一兒以日初出遠，而日中時近也。一兒曰："日初出大如車蓋；及日中，則如盤盂：此不為遠者小而近者大乎？"一兒曰："日初出滄滄涼涼；及日中如探湯：此不為近者熱而遠者涼乎？"孔子不能決也。兩小兒笑曰："孰為汝多知乎？"

《列子•湯問》

7. Far or Near

Confucius (551- 476 BC) saw two lads arguing as he was journeying eastward. He asked them what was the reason for their disagreement. One lad said, "I insist the sun is nearer to us when it rises in the morning, and it is farther away at noon." The other insisted that the sun was farther away when it rose, but nearer at noon.

The former lad argued, "When the sun rises, it's as big as the parasol suspended above one of the carriages. At noon it's as small as a plate. The nearer object must look bigger than the one farther away, mustn't it?"

The other replied, "When the sun rises, it's cold, but at noon it's hot. Doesn't the sun feel warmer when it is nearer?"

Confucius didn't know the answer to these questions and the two lads giggled and quipped, "Who is it who said you were so wise?"

Lie Zi (The Writings of Lie Yukou)

8. 魏王索鄭

　　魏王謂鄭王曰："始鄭、梁一國也，已而別，今願復得鄭而合之梁。"鄭君患之，召羣臣而與之謀所以對魏。鄭公子謂鄭君曰："此甚易應也。君對魏曰：'以鄭為故魏而可合也，則弊邑亦願得梁而合之鄭。'"魏王乃止。

《韓非子・內儲說》

8. The King of Wei Intends to Annex Zheng

The King of Wei[1] said to the King of Zheng, "Zheng and Liang[2] used to be parts of one state, and they split into different states later. I hope you join us to become one state again."

On hearing the request of the King of Wei, the King of Zheng was greatly worried. He called all his courtiers together to discuss the problem. The heir to the throne of Zheng suggested saying to the King of Wei in reply: "As you suppose that Zheng should join Wei, for they both were once parts of one state, we would like to incorporate Wei as well." After hearing this the King of Wei gave up the idea.

Han Fei Zi (The Writings of Han Fei)

---

(1) Wei: also called Liang ,a state in the Warring States Period (475-221BC) in Chinese history.
(2) Liang: another name of Wei.

9. 不死之藥

　　有獻不死之藥於荆王者，謁者操以入。中射之士問曰：“可食乎？”曰：“可。”因奪而食之。王怒，使人殺中射之士。中射之士使人説王曰：“臣問謁者，謁者曰：‘可食。’臣故食之。是臣無罪，罪在謁者也。且客獻不死之藥，臣食之而王殺之，是死藥也。王殺無罪之臣，而明人之欺王。”王乃不殺。

　　　　　　　　　　　　　　　　《韓非子‧説林》

9. The Elixir

Someone presented an elixir for eternal life to the King of the State of Jing[1]. While the courier was taking it to the King, one of the guards asked the courier if he would allow him to consume it instead. The courier agreed and so he swallowed the elixir.

When the King found this out, he was so angry that he ordered the guard be put to death. On hearing the command of the King, the guard asked somebody to plead his case on his behalf before the King, saying, "I asked the courier in the first place if he would allow me to take the elixir, and he agreed. Thus it is hardly myself who have offended you, but rather the courier. Secondly, the person who presented this elixir insisted that it would make you immortal. If you put me to death after I took it, surely it is not an elixir for eternal life after all, and you are being cheated. Then why should you put an innocent man to death like this?"

After the King heard the man's plea, he granted his pardon.

Han Fei Zi (The Writings of Han Fei)

---

(1) Jing: also called Chu, a state in the Spring and Autumn Period and the Warring States Period in Chinese history.

10. 知人不易

　　孔子窮乎陳蔡之間，藜羹不糂，七日不嘗粒。晝寢，顏回索米，得而炊之，幾熟，孔子望見顏回攫其甑中而食之。選間食熟，謁孔子而進食。孔子佯為不見之。孔子起曰："今者夢見先君，食潔而欲饋。"顏回對曰："不可，向者煤炱入甑中，棄食不祥，回攫而飯之。"孔子嘆曰："所信者目也，而目猶不可信；所恃者，心也，而心猶不足恃。弟子記之，知人固不易也。"

《呂氏春秋·審分覽·任數》

10. Not Easy to Know People

Confucius (551-476 BC) was in such adversity on his way from the State of Chen to that of Cai that he relieved his hunger with a soup of wild grass. He hadn't eaten a single grain of rice all week. As he was taking his nap at midday, Yan Hui (521-490 BC), a pupil of his, brought back some rice and began cooking it.

As the rice was almost done, Confucius saw Yan Hui eating some of it. When the rice was done, Yan Hui called Confucius to eat. Confucius pretended not to have seen anything, got up and said, "I dreamt of my late father, and I'd like to make an offering to his ghost with this meal." Yan Hui replied: "You can't, it's not pure. There was coal dust in the pot, but I thought it would be a pity to discard all the rice, so I picked out the dirty grains and ate them." At this, Confucius sighed and said, "I used to rely on my eyes to judge, but this time my eyes cannot be trusted; I used to rely on my heart to judge, but this time my heart fails me. Pupils, you should see it is not easy to understand somebody."

Lu Shi Chun Qiu (Lu's Annals)

27

11. 簫史

　　簫史者，秦穆公時人也。善吹簫，能致孔雀、白鶴
於庭。穆公有女，字弄玉，好之，公遂以女妻焉。日教
弄玉作鳳鳴。居數年，吹似鳳聲。鳳凰來止其屋，公為
作鳳臺，夫婦止其上。不下數年，一旦皆隨鳳凰飛去。
故秦人為作鳳女祠於雍宮中，時有簫聲而已。

　　　　　　　　　　　　　　　　劉向《列仙傳》

11. Xiao Shi

Xiao Shi, in the period of King Mu Gong (?- 621BC) of the State of Qin[1], was so adept at playing the *xiao*[2] that his music could attract the peacocks and white cranes to his courtyard. Mu Gong had a daughter, called Longyu, who was fond of the music. So Mu Gong married her to Xiao who made her sing like a phoenix day after day. After a few years, they were able to play the *xiao* so that it sounded like the call of the phoenix. As a result, a phoenix landed on their house eventually. Mu Gong constructed a phoenix hall to celebrate the event, and the couple had dwelt in it for several years when one day they flew away in the company of the phoenix. The folks of Qin built a temple for the "phoenix woman" in the Yong Palace. Since then the sound of the *xiao* can often be heard rising from around its eaves.

Liu Xiang (77-6BC)
Lie Xian Zhuan (Biography of Deities)

---

(1) Qin: a state in the Spring and Autumn Period (770-476 BC) in Chinese history.
(2) *xiao*: a vertical bamboo flute.

12. 桀紂並世

　　趙襄子飲酒，五日五夜不廢酒。謂侍者曰：“我誠邦士也！夫飲酒五日五夜矣，而殊不病。”優莫曰：“君勉之！不及紂二日耳。紂七日七夜，今君五日。”襄子懼，謂優莫曰：“然則吾亡乎？”優莫曰：“不亡。”襄子曰：“不及紂二日耳，不亡何待？”優莫曰：“桀、紂之亡也，遇湯、武，今天下盡桀也，而君紂也；桀紂並世，焉能相亡？然亦殆矣！”

劉向《新序》

12. Jie[1] and Zhou[2] Co-exist

King Xiang Zi of the State of Zhao had been enjoying his drink for five days and nights on end without getting drunk. He said to his servants, "I must be the greatest man in this State! I have been drinking for five days and nights, but I'm not sick yet."

You Mo replied to this: "You ought to take care of yourself! You are still two days and nights short of the record of Zhou, who drank for seven days and nights. Now you have already reached five."

King Xiang Zi was scared, and he asked You Mo, "Will my state perish like that of Zhou?" But You Mo replied, "The same will not occur."

"Only two days less than Zhou, how could my state not be subjugated as his was?" the King asked.

You Mo replied, "The fall of Jie and Zhou was attributed to Tang[3] and Wu[4] respectively. Nowadays there are only the Jies in power, and Your Majesty is like Zhou. Jie and Zhou exist simultaneously. How could they subjugate each other? However neither one is very far away from danger."

Liu Xiang (77-6BC)
Xin Xu (New Comments)

---

(1) Jie: the despotic last ruler of the Xia Dynasty (c. 22nd-17th C BC).
(2) Zhou: the despotic last ruler of the Shang Dynasty (17th-11th C BC).
(3) Tang: Tang defeated Jie and became the first emperor of the Shang Dynasty.
(4) Wu: Wu defeated Zhou and became the first emperor of the Zhou Dynasty (11thC-771BC).

13. 宗定伯賣鬼

　　南陽宗定伯，年少時，夜行逢鬼。問之，鬼言：
"我是鬼。"鬼問："汝復誰？"定伯誑之，言："我
亦鬼。"鬼問："欲至何所？"答曰："欲至宛市。"
鬼言："我亦欲至宛市。"遂行數里。鬼言："步行太
遲，可共遞相擔，何如？"定伯曰："大善。"鬼便先
擔定伯數里。鬼言："卿太重，將非鬼也？"定伯言：
"我新鬼，故身重耳。"定伯因復擔鬼，鬼略無重。如
是再三。定伯復言："我新鬼，不知有何所畏忌？"鬼
答言："惟不喜人唾。"於是共行，道遇水，定伯令鬼
先渡，聽之，了然無聲音。定伯自渡，漕灌作聲。鬼復
言："何以有聲？"定伯曰："新死，不習渡水故耳。
勿怪吾也。"行欲至宛市，定伯便擔鬼著肩上，急執
之，鬼大呼，聲咋咋然，索下，不復聽之。徑至宛市

13. Zong Dingbo Sells a Ghost

Zong Dingbo of Nanyang, when he was a young man, came across a ghost one night.

"Who are you?" Zong asked.

"A ghost," answered the ghost. "And you?"

"A ghost as well," lied Zong.

"Where are you going?"

"To the market of Wan."

"So am I."

They went along together for miles. The ghost suggested, "Walking like this is too slow. Why don't we take turns carrying each other?"

"Good idea!"

The ghost carried Zong first for a few miles.

"How heavy you are! Are you really a ghost?" the ghost asked.

"I'm a new one, so sort of heavy."

Then it was Zong's turn to carry the ghost, who was of no weight at all. They went on carrying each other in turn.

"As I died only recently," said Zong after some time, " I don't know what we spectres have to fear most."

"What we dread is human spittle."

They proceeded together till they came to a stream. Zong invited the ghost to cross first, who did it without a sound. Zong, however, made quite a splash.

"How come you made such a noise?" queried the ghost.

"I'm a new ghost, not accustomed yet to wading through water. Excuse me for that."

Approaching the market of Wan, Zong threw the ghost over his shoulder and held it fast. Yelling, the ghost begged to be put down, but Zong paid no attention, and made straight for the mar-

中，下著地，化為一羊，便賣之。恐其變化，唾之。得錢千五百乃去。

曹丕《列異傳》

ket. When he set the ghost down, it had turned into a sheep. Zong promptly sold it, having spat at it first to prevent it from changing into another form. Eventually Zong left the market, earning one thousand five hundred coins.

Cao Pei (187-226)
Lie Yi Zhuan (Records of Oddity)

14. 李冰

　　秦昭王使李冰為蜀守開成都縣兩江，溉田萬頃。神
須取女二人以為婦，冰自以女與神為婚，徑至祠勸神
酒，酒杯澹澹，因厲聲責之，因忽不見。良久，有兩蒼
牛鬪於江岸，有間，輒還，流汗謂官屬曰：「吾鬪疲
極，不當相助耶？南向腰中正白者，我綬也。」主簿刺
殺北面者，江神遂死。

應劭《風俗通》

14. Li Bing Kills the River God

King Zhao (324-251BC) of the State of Qin promoted Li Bing to the post of magistrate of Shu. He ordered him to build a dyke off the Min River in Chengdu to irrigate the ten thousand hectares of fields in that area. The river god wanted two virgins to become his wives, and Li Bing wished to offer his own daughters to the god. He went to the temple to have a drink with the god and to offer him his daughters. As they were drinking, they began to argue fiercely about the matter and suddenly they both disappeared.

After a good while there appeared two black buffaloes wrestling by the river. After some time Li Bing returned in a sweat, and he informed his subordinates, " I'm nearly exhausted from fighting him, why wouldn't you help me? The buffalo on the south side with a white ribbon around its waist is me." Then he went back to fight with the river god again. His lieutenant stabbed the buffalo standing on the north side, and so put to death the river god.

Ying Shao
Feng Cu Tong (Legends)

15. 趙伯公醉臥

　　趙伯公肥大，夏日醉臥，孫兒緣其肚上戲，因以李子內其臍中，累七八枚；既醉，了不覺；數日後，乃知痛。李大爛，汁出，以為臍穴，懼死，乃命妻子處分家事，泣謂家人曰："我腸爛將死。"明日李核出，乃知孫兒所內李子也。

邯鄲淳《笑林》

15. Fatty Zhao Gets Drunk

Zhao Bogong was enormously fat. One summer day he slept after having got drunk. His grandchildren played round his belly and stuffed seven or eight plums in his belly button. He was too drunk to be aware of it. A couple of days later, he felt a pain in his belly. The plums were all rotten, with the juice oozing out. Zhao thought his belly had leaked and was quite afraid that his end was coming. He told his wife how to arrange the household after his death and said to his family in tears, "My intestines are rotten. I'm dying." The next day, the plum stones dropped out, and he finally realized that they were simply some rotten plums which had been put into his belly button by his grandchildren.

Handan Chun
Xiao Lin (A Collection of Jests)

16. 天河浮槎

　　舊説云：“天河與海通”。近世有人居海渚者，年年八月有浮槎，去來不失期。人有奇志，立飛閣於槎上，多齎糧，乘槎而去。十餘日中猶觀星月日辰；自後芒芒忽忽，亦不覺晝夜。去十餘日，奄至一處，有城郭狀，屋舍甚嚴，遙望宮中多織婦。見一丈夫牽牛渚次飲之，牽牛人乃驚問曰：“何由至此？”此人見説來意，並問此是何處。答曰：“君還，至蜀郡訪嚴君平[1] 則知之。”竟不上岸，因還如期。乃至蜀問君平。曰：“某年月日有客星犯牽牛宿。”計年月日，正是此人到天河時也。

　　　　　　　　　　　　　　　張華《博物志》

---

(1) 嚴君平：西漢隱士，賣卜於成都市。

16. Rafting on the Heavenly River[1]

The old saying goes: " The Heavenly River connects with the sea." Not long ago there was a man living on the beach. He saw a raft appear in the sea on exactly the same day in August every year. This man had an ambition to float along the Heavenly River. He set up a cabin on the raft and drifted away with a lot of food in store. During the first dozen days or so he could still distinguish the moon and the sun, but afterwards he was dazed, and could not tell night from day. After another dozen days he reached a place, where there were city walls and grand buildings. In a palace in the distance, many women could be seen weaving.

A man leading a buffalo to the water caught sight of this outsider and asked him in surprise, " How did you come here?" The outsider described how he came and enquired where it was he had arrived. The other's reply was: " Please go back to Chengdu and visit the hermit and seer Yan Jun Ping, then you will have the answer." So, the man didn't go ashore but returned. When he arrived at Chengdu, he consulted Yan Jun Ping, who replied: "One day a guest star disturbed the Buffalo Star[2]." On counting the days, they discovered that it was exactly the day when the man reached the shore of the Heavenly River on the raft.

Zhang Hua (232-300)
Bo Wu Zhi (Records of Myriad Things)

---

(1) Heavenly River: the Milky Way.
(2) Buffalo Star: the Altair.

17. 馬太守

　　興古太守馬氏在官，有親故人投之求恤焉。馬乃令此人出外住，詐云：是神人道士，治病無不手下立愈。又令辯士遊行，為之虛聲，云：能令盲者明，躄者即行。於是四方雲集，趨之如市，而錢帛固已山積矣。又敕諸來治病者，雖不便愈，其當告人已愈也。如此則必愈也；若告人言未愈者，則後終不愈也。道法正爾，不可不承信。於是後人問前來者，輒告之云已愈，不敢言未愈者也。旬日之間，乃致巨富焉。

　　　　　　　　　　　　　　　葛洪《抱朴子》

17. Prefect Ma and the Quack

When Prefect Ma of Xinggu was still in his post, a relative of his came and asked him for help. Ma found somewhere for him to live and gave out the false information that this man was a magic Taoist priest who had supernatural power to cure all diseases instantly. Then Ma had a glib gossiper spread the rumour in the street that this priest was able to cure blindness and cause the lame to walk. Consequently people flocked to him from all around, as if to a fair, and the money he grabbed began piling up.

The priest warned his gullible patients that even if they were not cured, they should yet declare themselves well, as they would thus certainly regain their health. But if they did not do so, they would never recover. He taught them that this was one of the principles of healing in which they must believe.

Thus, when a patient was asked by another about his recovery, the former would declare that he was well, daring not to tell the truth. After not many days this quack had already amassed great wealth.

Ge Hong (284-363)
Bao Pu Zi

18. 漢高建新豐

　　太上皇徙長安，居深宮，悽愴不樂。高祖[1]竊因左右間其故。以平生所好，皆屠販少年，沽酒賣餅，鬥雞蹴踘，以此為歡；今皆無此，故以不樂。高祖乃作新豐，移諸故人實之，太上皇乃悅。故新豐多無賴，無衣冠子弟故也。高祖少時，常祭枌榆之社，及移新豐，亦還立焉。高帝既作新豐，並移舊社，衢巷棟宇，物色惟舊。士女老幼，相攜路首，各知其室。放犬羊雞鴨於通途，亦競識其家。其匠人胡寬所營也。移者皆悅其似而德之，故競加賞贈，月餘致累百金。

葛洪《西京雜記》

---

(1) 漢高祖：劉邦。死後上尊號為高皇帝，故稱。

18. Emperor Gaozu Builds Xinfeng

The father of Emperor Gaozu (?-188BC) of the Han Dynasty moved to the capital Chang'an[1] from his hometown Feng and lived in the palace. He was quite unhappy after that. The Emperor asked those close to his father in private what might be the cause. They told him that when his father was in Feng, he got along with young butchers and hawkers who were interested in selling liquor, peddling cakes, holding cock-fights and playing ball games. Now that all this was over, he felt depressed. The Emperor gave a command to construct a new district, called Xinfeng[2], in Chang'an and had old folks in Feng move to the district. His father cheered up at last. That was the reason why ever since a great number of vagrants lived in the Xinfeng District, but not gentlemen.

When the Emperor was young, he often made sacrifices at a temple for mother earth in Feng. So he had an identical temple built in the new district as well. When Xinfeng and the temple were completed, the streets and the buildings were all the same as those of the old Feng. As the folks from Feng strolled in the streets, they would have no difficulty in recognizing their old houses. Driving their livestock along the lanes, they could find their own homes without hesitation as well. All the folks who moved here were pleased with the resemblance and praised the architect Hu Kuan. They rewarded him a lot for it, and in a month or so he received a hundred ounces of gold.

Ge Hong (284-363)
Xi Jing Za Ji (Western Capital Miscellanies)

---

(1) Chang'an: an ancient Chinese capital, now Xi'an.
(2) Xinfeng: meaning a new Feng in Chinese.

19. 鷫鸘裘

　　司馬相如（長卿）與卓文君還成都，居貧愁懣，以所著鷫鸘裘就市人陽昌貰酒，與文君為歡。既而文君抱頸而泣曰：“我平生富足，今乃以衣裘貰酒！”遂相與謀，於成都賣酒。相如親著犢鼻褌滌器，以恥王孫[1]。王孫果以為病，乃厚給文君，文君遂為富人。文君姣好，眉色如望遠山，臉際常若芙蓉，肌膚柔滑如脂。十七而寡，為人放誕風流，故悅長卿之才而越禮焉。長卿素有消渴疾，及還成都，悅文君之色，遂以發痼疾。乃作美人賦，欲以自刺，而終不能改，卒以此疾至死。文君為誄，傳於世。

葛洪《西京雜記》

---

(1) 王孫：卓王孫，文君父，成都豪富。

19. The Feather Coat

After Sima Xiangru[1] and his wife Zhuo Wenjun returned to Chengdu, they were overcome by poverty. One day they exchanged Wenjun's peacock feather coat with a businessman, called Yang Chang, for a hearty drink. However, Wenjun hugged Xiangru's neck and cried, " I used to live a well-off life, but today I had to exchange my coat for a drink!" Then they decided to run a tiny shop in Chengdu to sell liquor. Xiangru wore an apron and washed the vessels and dishes himself in order to shame Wangsun (Wenjun's father, a rich man). Before long, as they expected, Wangsun felt bad about it and sent Wenjun a good fortune. So they turned rich again.

Wenjun was beautiful. Her eyebrows looked like the curve of distant hills, her cheeks were just like a cottonrose hibiscus (Hibiscus mutabilis) in full bloom, and her skin was as soft and smooth as cream. She was bereaved of her husband at the age of seventeen, but being a dissolute woman, she later carried on a clandestine love affair with Xiangru instead of living in widowhood, for she admired his talent. Xiangru had had diabetes for a long time. After he came back to Chengdu, he admired Wenjun's beauty and made merry with her . This caused his illness to relapse. He composed a "Fu[2] on Beauties" to caution himself. Nevertheless he just couldn't help things, and at last he died of the diabetes. Wenjun wrote an epitaph on him, which has been handed down ever since.

Ge Hong (284-363)
Xi Jing Za Ji (Western Capital Miscellanies)

---

(1) Sima Xiangru (179BC-117BC) of the Han Dynasty was famous for his writings.
(2) *Fu*: a descriptive prose interspersed with verse.

20. 王嬙[1]

　　元帝（公元前48-33）後宮既多，不得常見，乃使畫工圖形，案圖召幸之。諸宮人皆賂畫工，多者十萬，少者亦不減五萬。獨王嬙不肯，遂不得見。後匈奴入朝，求美人為閼氏。於是上案圖，以昭君行。及去，召見，貌為後宮第一，善應對，舉止嫻雅。帝悔之，而名籍已定。帝重信於外國，故不復更人，乃窮案其事，畫工皆棄市，籍其家資皆巨萬。畫工有杜陵毛延壽，為人

---

(1) 王嬙：即王昭君。

20. A Beauty's Tragedy

Emperor Yuan (48-33BC) of the Han Dynasty had too many concubines and maids of honour in the palace to see them often. So he ordered painters to draw portraits of them and called on them according to the portraits.

All the concubines and the maids of honour bribed the painters so as to be drawn as pretty as pretty could be. The highest offer was a hundred thousand coppers, even the lowest was not less than fifty thousand. But Wang Qiang (Zhaojun)[1] was not willing to do so, therefore she was never called on by the Emperor.

Later an envoy of Hun[2] visited the court and requested for a beauty to be the Hunnish Queen. Displaying the portraits, Emperor Yuan decided to let Zhaojun go. Just before she was about to leave, the Emperor interviewed her and found her looks more beautiful than any other concubines and maids, her answers properly worded and her bearing elegant. The Emperor regretted deeply having to let her go. However, the deal was already made with the King of Hun. As he kept his word to foreigners always, he would not change his mind. But he had the case investigated and all the painters executed. By searching their houses, huge fortunes were exposed. Among the painters killed was Mao Yanshou from Duling, who was especially skilled at painting portraits which always bore a striking resemblance to the real persons, no matter

---

(1) Wang Qiang: alias Wang Zhaojun, was a maid of honour in the palace of the Han Dynasty, thought to be one of the prominent beauties in Chinese history. She was ordered to be married to the King of Hun. Her tragic experience later became the theme of drama.
(2) Hun: an ancient state founded by the Huns in Mongolia.

形，醜好老少，必得其真；安陵陳敞，新豐劉白、龔
寬，並工為牛馬飛鳥眾勢，人形好醜，不逮延壽；下杜
陽望亦善畫，尤善布色，樊育亦善布色；同日棄市。京
師畫工，於是差稀。

葛洪《西京雜記》

whether they were ugly or pretty, old or young. Other painters like Chen Chang from Anling, Liu Bai and Gong Kuan from Xinfeng, were all good at painting cattle, horses and birds in all poses and also human beings, though they could not match Mao. Yang Wang, from Xiadu, was also adept at painting, especially with colour, and so was Fan Yu. As they were executed at the same time, it was rare to meet a good painter in the capital since then.

Ge Hong (284-363)
Xi Jing Za Ji (Western Capital Miscellanies)

21. 河間男女

　　晉武帝[1]世，河間郡有男女私悦，許相配適。尋而男從軍，積年不歸。女家更欲適之。女不願行，父母逼之，不得已而去。尋病死。其男戍還，問女所在。其家具説之。乃至冢，欲哭之盡哀，而不勝其情。遂發冢開棺，女即蘇活，因負還家。將養數日，平復如初。後夫聞，乃往求之。其人不還，曰：“卿婦已死，天下豈聞死人可復活耶？此天賜我，非卿婦也。”於是相訟。郡縣不能決，以讞廷尉。秘書郎王導奏：“以精誠之至，感於天地，故死而更生。此非常事，不得以常禮斷之。請還開冢者。”朝廷從其議。

干寶《搜神記》

---

(1) 晉武帝：司馬炎。

21. A Man and a Woman of Hejian

In the period of Emperor Wu (?-290) of the Jin Dynasty, there were a man and a woman in Hejian County who fell in love and vowed to marry each other. Later the man enlisted in the army for years without coming back. The woman's parents urged her to get married, and at last she was forced to marry another man reluctantly. Before long she died of an illness.

As soon as the man retired from the frontier, he asked where the woman was. His family described to him what had happened. By her tomb, he wept himself out, but even wailing could not relieve his deep sorrow. He dug out the tomb and opened the coffin, at which instant the woman was brought back to life.

The man carried her home. Having been nursed carefully, the woman regained her health. Her husband, hearing of it, requested the woman back. The man refused him: "Your wife has already died. Have you ever heard of the resurrection of the dead? She is not your wife, but a gift granted to me by Heaven."

They went to court against each other. The heads of the county could not decide on the case, so they appealed to the Imperial Court. The Secretary of State Wang Tao (276—339) presented a memorial to the Emperor: "This man and woman moved Heaven by their sincerity, that's why she was brought back to life. It's not an ordinary case, we may not settle it according to the ordinary law. Let the man who dug out the tomb have the woman." The Emperor followed his suggestion.

Gan Bao
Sou Shen Ji (Fairy Tales)

22. 干將莫邪（三王墓）

　　楚干將莫邪為楚王作劍，三年乃成。王怒，欲殺之。劍有雌雄。其妻重身當產，夫語妻曰："吾為王作劍，三年乃成。王怒，往必殺我。汝若生子是男，大，告之曰：'出戶望南山，松生石上，劍在其背。'"於是即將雌劍，往見楚王。王大怒，使相之："劍有二，一雄一雌。雌來雄不來。"王怒，即殺之。莫邪子名赤，比後壯，乃問其母："吾父所在？"母曰："汝父為楚王作劍，三年乃成。王怒，殺之。去時囑我：'語汝子：出戶望南山，松生石上，劍在其背。'"於是子出戶南望，不見有山，但覩堂前松柱下，石砥之上，即以斧破其背，得劍。日夜思欲報楚王。王夢見一兒，眉間廣尺，言："欲報讎。"王即購之千金。兒聞之，

22. Ganjiang and Moya (Three King's Grave)

Ganjiang and Moya, a couple of the State of Chu, were required to make a pair of swords for the King. They spent three years in producing them. The King was annoyed for the delay and intended to kill the husband. The pair of swords were made up of a female and a male.

The wife Moya had long been pregnant and was about to labour. The husband told her, "Since it took us three years long to make the swords, the King must be mad at me. When I go to him, he must kill me. If the baby is a boy, when he grows up, tell him to go out of the door and look up towards the South Hill. There will be a pine growing at a rock, and a sword will be at its back."

Then he called on the King with the female sword. The King flew into a rage, having the sword checked; "There ought to have been a couple, but the male one is missing!" The King cut up nasty, and had Ganjiang killed.

When Ganjiang's son, named Chi, reached maturity, he asked his mother, "Where's my father?" The reply was, "Your father made swords for the King, but it took him three years. The enraged King killed him. Before he left for the King, he urged me to tell you to go out of the door and look up towards the South Hill. There will be a pine on a rock, and a sword is at its back."

The son went out and looked southwards. He did not find the hill but saw a pine growing on the stone pedestal in front of the house. He chopped at it with an axe and got the male sword. From then on he swore vengeance against the King day and night.

One day the King dreamed of a boy with eyebrows wide apart, who declared revenge on him. The King offered a reward of a thousand ounces of gold for the capture of the boy. The son, hav-

亡去。入山行歌。客有逢者，謂：“子年少，何哭之甚悲耶？”曰：“吾干將莫邪子也。楚王殺吾父，吾欲報之！”客曰：“聞王購子頭千金，將子頭與劍來，為子報之。”兒曰：“幸甚！”即自刎，兩手捧頭及劍奉之，立僵。客曰：“不負子也。”於是屍乃仆。客持頭往見楚王，王大喜。客曰：“此乃勇士頭也。當於湯鑊煮之。”王如其言。煮頭三日三夕，不爛。頭踔出湯中，瞋目大怒。客曰：“此兒頭不爛，願王自往臨視之，是必爛也。”王即臨之。客以劍擬王，王頭隨墮湯中。客亦自擬己頭，頭復墮湯中。三首俱爛，不可識別。乃分其湯肉葬之，故通名“三王墓”。今在汝南北宜春縣界。

干寶《搜神記》

ing heard of it, fled. One day while he was singing a dirge in the mountains, a stranger came across him, and asked, "You're so young, why are you crying so sorrowfully?"

"I'm the son of Ganjiang, the King of Chu killed my father. I'm going to avenge my father."

The stranger said, "I hear that the King is offering a thousand ounces of gold for your head. If you let me have your head and the sword, I'll seek revenge for you."

"Done!" the son said. He cut off his head in no time and handed the head and the sword to the stranger while his body stood there stiffly. The stranger said, "I'll not let you down." No sooner had he finished his words than the son fell down, dead.

The stranger took Chi's head to the King of Chu, and the King was very glad. The stranger said, "It's the head of a hero, you should boil it in a pot." The King did accordingly. Three days had passed, nevertheless the head did not melt, but bounded up above the water, glowering with fury. The stranger said, "The head has not dissolved. If Your Majesty come over and stare down at it, then it will melt away." As the King came over to look at it, the stranger swiped at him with the sword, and the head of the King dropped into the boiling water at once.Then the stranger chopped off his own head which also dropped into the pot. The three heads were soon disfigured beyond all recognition.

People divided the broth into three portions and buried them together in one grave, and called it "Three Kings' Grave", which is today found in Yichun County, north of Runan.

Gan Bao
Sou Shen Ji (Fairy Tales)

23. 五柳先生傳

　　先生不知何許人也，亦不詳其姓字。宅邊有五柳樹，因以為號焉。閑靜少言，不慕榮利。好讀書，不求甚解；每有會意，便欣然忘食。性嗜酒，家貧不能常得。親舊知其如此，或置酒而招之。造飲輒盡，期在必醉；既醉而退，曾不吝情去留。環堵蕭然，不蔽風日。短褐穿結，簞瓢屢空。晏如也。常著文章自娛，頗示己志。忘懷得失，以此自終。

陶潛《陶淵明集》

23. Mr. "Five Willows" [1]

No one knew where this gentleman came from and what his name was. There were five willows by his house, therefore he was named Mr. "Five Willows". He was quiet and reserved, not envious of high position or great wealth. He enjoyed reading, but never tried hard to look for deeper meanings. Each time when he caught the point in a book, he would be in such high spirits that he would simply forget to have dinner. He was very fond of drink but was too poor to drink often. His old friends knew it, so they often invited him to have wine. He always drank to the bottom and got drunk. Then he took his leave, and nobody minded.

For his whole life, he dwelled in a humble house, had scanty clothing, and always lacked food, but he lived in peace. Sometimes he entertained himself by writing to show his ideals, and he never cared for gain or loss.

Tao Qian (365-427)
Tao Yuanming Ji (Collected Works of Tao Yuanming)

---

(1) Mr. "Five Willows": pseudonym of Tao Yuanming (Tao Qian), famous poet of the Eastern Jin Dynasty (317-420). In this piece, the poet is describing himself.

24. 楊生狗

　　晉太和中，廣陵人楊生，養一狗，甚愛憐之，行止與俱。後生飲酒醉。行大澤草中，眠不能動。時方冬月燎原，風勢極盛。狗乃周章號喚，生醉不覺。前有一坑水，狗便走往水中，還，以身灑生左右草上。如此數次，周旋跬步，草皆沾濕，火至免焚。生醒方見之。爾後，生因暗行，墮於空井中。狗呻吟徹曉。有人經過，怪此狗向井號，往視，見生。生曰：“君可出我，當有厚報。”人曰：“以此狗見與，便當相出。”生曰：“此狗曾活我已死，不得相與。餘即無惜。”人曰：“若爾，便不相出。”狗因下頭目井。生知其意，乃語

24. A Faithful Dog

During the Tai He period (366-371) of the Jin Dynasty, there was a young man named Yang living in Guang Ling. He possessed a dog, which he was very fond of. Wherever he went the dog followed.

One day on his way through the marshes, Yang was so drunk that he fell down and was soon asleep. It was winter, and it happened that the grass was so dry that it caught fire. As the wind fanned the flames higher and higher, the dog rushed around Yang, barking frantically in order to wake him. Yang however was too drunk to wake up. At this stage the dog jumped into the marsh water and wet itself. It then came over to where Yang lay and rolled on the grass around him. The dog repeated this action several times until the grass was thoroughly soaked, and Yang was saved from the fire. It was not until he awoke that he realized what had happened.

On another occasion Yang was out after dark, and fell into a disused well. The dog howled and growled around the well all night until a passer-by noticed it barking and walked over to discover Yang in the well. Yang begged the man, saying, "If you help me get out of here, I promise you a good reward." To this the man responded: "If you promise me your dog I'll help you." Yang replied, "How can I let you take my dog? He has saved me many times and I owe my life to him." At this the stranger retorted, "If you don't agree, I'll just leave you in the well."

The dog at that moment peered over the side of the well and stared down at its master. It occurred to Yang that the dog was giving him a signal. So he shouted his agreement to the request of the stranger.

路人云"以狗相與。"人即出之，繫之而去。卻後五日，狗夜走歸。

陶潛《搜神後記》

The man helped Yang out of the well, and placing a rope around the dog's neck, he led it away. After five days, the dog returned to its old master in the night.

Tao Qian (365-427)
Sou Shen Hou Ji (A Sequel to Gan Bao's Fairy Tales)

25. 小時了了

　　孔文舉[1]年十歲，隨父到洛。時李元禮[1]有盛名，為司隸校尉[2]。詣門者皆儁才清稱及中表親戚，乃通。文舉至門，謂吏曰："我是李府君親。"既通，前坐。元禮問曰："君與僕有何親？"對曰："昔先君仲尼與君先人伯陽有師資之尊，是僕與君奕世為通好也。"元禮及賓客莫不奇之。太中大夫[3]陳韙後至，人以其語語之，韙曰："小時了了，大未必佳。"文舉曰："想君小時，必當了了。"韙大踧踖。

劉義慶《世說新語》

---

(1) 孔文舉：孔融，字文舉；李膺，字元禮，皆漢末人。
(2) 司隸校尉：東漢時掌管洛陽京都司法及公安官員。
(3) 太中大夫：漢因秦制設置，後漢有二十人，是直屬皇帝的散官，掌論議。

25. Smart When Young

Kong Wenju (153-208) came to Luoyang with his father when he was ten. At that time Li Yuanli (110-169) was in charge of the Judicature and Public Security and enjoyed great prestige in Luoyang. Only prominent figures or his close relatives were allowed to visit him. Wenju approached his gate and said to the doorman, "I'm a relative of Mr.Li." So he was allowed in. When he sat down, Li asked him, "How is it that you are a relative of mine?" The reply was: "Long ago, my ancestor Confucius[1] called your ancestor Laozi[2] by the title of Master, therefore you and I have a relationship spanning many generations." Li and other guests present wondered at him.

When Chen Wei, an adviser of the Emperor, came later, others told him the words of the boy, but he uttered, "Being smart at a young age doesn't mean he'll be a somebody when he grows up." Kong answered on the instant, "I'm sure you must be smart when you were young." Chen was choked up.

Liu Yiqing (403-444)
Shi Shuo Xin Yu (New Accounts of Old Episodes)

---

(1) Confucius' family name was Kong, same as Wenju's.
(2) Laozi's family name was Li, same as Yuanli's.

26. 坦腹東牀

　　郗太傅[1] 在京口，遣門生與王丞相[2] 書，求女婿。丞相語郗信：“君往東廂，任意選之。”門生歸，白郗曰：“王家諸郎，亦皆可嘉，聞來覓婿，咸自矜持。唯有一郎，在牀上坦腹臥，如不聞。”郗公云：“正此好！”訪之，乃是逸少[3]，因嫁女與焉。

劉慶義《世說新語》

---

(1) 郗太傅：郗鑒。
(2) 王丞相：王導。
(3) 逸少：王羲之（303－361）字。東晉大書法家，為丞相王導從子。

26. Choosing a Son-in-law

The Emperor's adviser Xi Jian (269-339), while in Jing Kou, sent one of his associates to present a letter to the Premier Wang, stating that he wished to have one of Wang's sons as a son-in-law. When the Premier heard this request, he said to the messenger, "Why don't you go out to the eastern wing-room where my sons are and take a look?"

When the messenger returned to Jing Kou, he reported to Xi Jian, "The young Wangs are all suitable men. Yet when I arrived to look for a son-in-law for you they all became tense and uneasy. There was however one exception, he just lay on his back with his belly uncovered, nonchalant as if he knew nothing of the purpose of my visit." At this Xi Jian replied, "That one will do fine."

After inquiring further, he discovered that the young man's name was Wang Xizhi (303-361)[1], and he decided to marry his daughter to him.

Liu Yiqing (403-444)
Shi Shuo Xin Yu (New Accounts of Old Episodes)

---

(1) Wang Xizhi: a famous calligrapher of the Eastern Jin Dynasty in Chinese history.

27. 周處自新

　　周處年少時，兇彊俠氣，為鄉里所患。又義興水中有蛟，山中有邅跡虎，並皆暴犯百姓，義興人謂為三橫，而處尤劇。或説處殺虎斬蛟，實冀三橫唯餘其一。處即刺殺虎，又入水擊蛟，蛟或浮或沒，行數十里，處與之俱。經三日三夜，鄉里皆謂已死，更相慶，竟殺蛟而出。聞里人相慶，始知為人情所患，有自改意。乃自吳尋二陸[1]，平原不在，正見清河，具以情告，並云："欲自修改，而年已蹉跎，終無所成。"清河曰："古

⑴ 二陸：陸機（261—301）、陸雲（262—303）兄弟，機官平原內
　　史，雲官清河內史。周處比二陸大二十多歲，這個故事説他
　　"自吳尋二陸"而"改勵"，不可靠。

27. Zhou Chu Starts a New Life

When he was a young man, Zhou Chu (240-299) was tough and fond of fighting. Residents of Yi Xing, his hometown, both feared and hated him.

At that time there was in the district a terrible monster known as the *jiao*[1], which lived in the river, and a man-eating tiger that lived in the mountains. Together with Zhou Chu, they were known as the "three terrors" plaguing the people. And Zhou Chu was considered to be the worst.

At one time somebody persuaded Zhou Chu to go and kill the other two monsters, in the hope that he might be killed in the struggle. He agreed to the request. After slaughtering the tiger in the mountains, he jumped into the river and launched an attack on the *jiao*. The *jiao* sometimes rose to the surface and sometimes swam in the depth of the river, while Zhou Chu followed it for tens of miles all along. Three days and nights had passed, the residents decided that Zhou Chu must have already been eaten by the *jiao*, and they had a celebration.

At this time, Zhou Chu succeeded in killing the *jiao* and re-emerged from the river. Knowing what the people were celebrating, he at last realized how deeply hated he had become. So he decided to start a new life, and went off in search of two scholars, known as the Lu brothers, for advice.

Lu Ji (261-301) was out at that time, but his young brother, Lu Yun (262-303), was at home. Zhou Chu recounted the recent events to him and said, "I wish to correct my behaviour, but I am no longer young, and change will not come easy."

---

(1) *jiao*: a kind of crocodile.

人貴朝聞夕死，況君前途尚可。且人患志之不立，亦何憂令名不彰邪？”處遂改勵，終為忠臣孝子。

劉義慶《世説新語》

Lu Yun replied, "Confucius once said that if you found out the truth in the morning but died the same evening, you would feel no regret. You are still young and have a life of promise ahead of you. What you should fear is having no goal in your life. If you already have one, why worry that you will never come to fame?"

From then on Zhou Chu made great efforts to turn over a new leaf, and later was applauded as a loyal official and a loving son.

Liu Yiqing (403-444)
Shi Shuo Xin Yu (New Accounts of Old Episodes)

28. 雪夜訪戴[1]

　　王子猷[2]居山陰，夜大雪，眠覺，開室，命酌酒。四望皎然，因起仿偟，詠左思[3]招隱詩。忽憶戴安道，時戴在剡，即便夜乘小船就之。經宿方至，造門不前而返。人問其故，王曰："吾本乘興而行，興盡而返，何必見戴？"

　　　　　　　　　　劉義慶《世說新語》

(1) 戴：戴逵（？—395），字安道。東晉時隱居剡縣。
(2) 王子猷：王徽之（？—約386），字子猷，羲之子。任性放達。
(3) 左思：晉著名詩人。其招隱詩云："杖策招隱士，荒途橫古今。巖穴無結構，丘中有鳴琴，白雲停陰岡，丹葩曜陽林。"

28. A Visit on a Snowy Night

Wang Ziyou (?- ca.386) lived in Shan Yin. One night while it was snowing heavily, he got up from his bed, opened the door, and told his servant to bring some wine. Looking outside, he found that everything within sight was covered by a shimmering layer of snow. Feeling a little restless, he paced up and down his room, reciting the "Ode to the Recluse" by Zuo Si. Suddenly his friend Dai Andao, who lived in Shan, came to his mind. He decided to pay him a visit by boat that very night. On reaching Dai's door-steps, he ordered the boatman to return home, without disembarking to see his friend.

Somebody, puzzled by this act, asked Wang Ziyou the reason for his behaviour. He replied, "I set out in high spirits, and returned after a thoroughly enjoyable trip. Why bother to go in to see Dai?"

Liu Yiqing (403-444)
Shi Shuo Xiu Yu (New Accounts of Old Episodes)

29. 未能忘情

　　張玄之、顧敷，是顧和中外孫[1]，皆少而聰惠。和並知之，而常謂顧勝，親重偏至，張頗不懨。於時張年九歲，顧年七歲，和與俱至寺中。見佛般泥洹[2]像，弟子有泣者，有不泣者，和以問二孫。玄謂："被親故泣，不被親故不泣。"敷曰："不然，當由忘情故不泣，不能忘情故泣。"

劉義慶《世說新語》

---

(1) 中外孫：孫與外孫的合稱。孫不能單稱中孫。
(2) 般泥洹：涅槃的異譯，佛教說死為涅槃。

29. Not Above Earthly Emotions

Gu He (288-351) had two grandsons, Zhang Xuanzhi, the son of his daughter, and Gu Fu, his son's son. When they were young they were both very bright. Gu He often said that Gu Fu was smarter, and loved him more than he loved Zhang Xuanzhi, and the latter felt hurt by this.

When Zhang Xuanzhi was nine and Gu Fu seven years old, Gu He took them to a temple, where they saw the sculptures of the Buddha's death. Some of the Buddha's disciples were depicted as weeping whilst others were not, so Gu He asked his grandsons why this was so.

Zhang Xuanzhi replied, "Those loved by the Buddha wept, while those not loved did not."

To this, Gu Fu disagreed, saying, "Not at all. Those who had forgotten their emotions did not weep, while those who were not above emotions wept!"

Liu Yiqing (403-444)
Shi Shuo Xin Yu (New Accounts of Old Episodes)

30. 荀巨伯

　　荀巨伯遠看友人疾。值胡賊攻郡，友人語巨伯曰：
"吾今死矣，子可去。"巨伯曰："遠來相視，子今吾
去，敗義以求生，豈荀巨伯所行耶！"賊既至，謂巨伯
曰：　"大軍至，一郡盡空。汝何男子，而敢獨止？"
巨伯曰："友人有疾，不忍委之。寧以我身，代友人
命。"賊相謂曰："我輩無義之人，而入有義之國！"
遂班軍而還，一郡並獲全。

　　　　　　　　　　　　　　　劉義慶《世說新語》

30. A Faithful Friend

Xun Jubo travelled far to visit a friend who was badly ill. In that period the Hun[1] invaders were making an attack on the county in which his friend lived. The friend said to Xun, "I'm dying, please go." Xun said, "I came a long distance to see you, but you want me to leave. Being disloyal to a friend only to save myself is an unrighteous act that is beneath me."

The invaders arrived at last and asked Xun, "Our troops are coming, all the people in the county have fled. But what kind of man are you, who dare to remain here alone?"

"My friend is terribly sick," Xun said. "I can't bear to leave him alone. I prefer to be killed in his place." The invaders said to themselves, "We are unrighteous. How can we make an attempt on a righteous county?" Then they withdrew the troops and the whole county was saved.

Liu Yiqing (403-444)
Shi Shuo Xin Yu (New Accounts of Old Episodes)

---

(1) Hun: see Note 2 on paqe 49.

31. 劉伶戒酒

　　劉伶[1]病酒，渴甚，從婦求酒。婦捐酒毀器，涕泣諫曰：「君飲太過，非攝生之道，必宜斷之！」伶曰：「甚善。我不能自禁，唯當祝鬼神，自誓斷之耳！便可具酒肉。」婦曰：「敬聞命。」供酒肉於神前，請伶祝誓。伶跪而祝曰：「天生劉伶，以酒為名，一飲一斛，五斗解酲。婦人之言，慎不可聽。」便引酒進肉，隗然已醉矣。

劉義慶《世説新語》

---

(1) 劉伶：晉人，與阮籍 (210 - 263) 等稱竹林七賢。

31. An Alcoholic Takes the Pledge

Liu Ling was thirsty for drink one day, so he asked his wife for wine. After throwing out all the wine and destroying all the drinking vessels, his wife begged him in tears: "You drink too hard, it's not good for your health. Please give it up!"

Liu Ling replied, "All right, but I find it very hard to make this commitment. So let us sacrifice to the gods and beg for their help, then I'll take the pledge. You go and prepare the wine and meat for the sacrifice."

The wife replied, "I comply with your wish." Then she laid out the wine and meat for the gods, and told Liu Ling to pledge his word.

Liu Ling knelt, saying to the gods, "I was born for drink. With one gulp I could down a whole *hu*[1], another five *dou*[2] would make me sober. Don't pay any attention to what this woman says." Then he finished off the wine and meat, and soon he was drunk.

Liu Yiqing (403-444)
Shi Shuo Xin Yu (New Accounts of Old Episodes)

---

(1) 1 *hu*=10 *dou*
(2) 1 *dou*=10 litres

32. 溫嶠娶婦

溫公喪婦。從姑劉氏，家值亂離散；唯有一女，甚有姿慧，姑以屬公覓婚。公密有自婚意，答曰："佳婿難得，但如嶠比云何？"姑云："喪敗之餘，乞粗存活，便足慰吾餘年，何敢希汝比。"卻後少日，公報姑云："已覓得婚處。門地粗可，婿身名宦，盡不減嶠。"因下玉鏡台一枚。姑大喜，既婚交禮，女以手披紗扇，撫掌大笑曰："我固疑是老奴，果如所卜。"

劉義慶《世説新語》

32. Wen Jiao Gets Married

The revered Mr. Wen Jiao (288-329) was bereaved of his wife. At that time the family of his aunt, Mrs. Liu, was forced to leave their hometown which was broken up by the war. There was only a daughter, pretty and intelligent, still living with her. The aunt trusted Mr. Wen to seek a husband for her daughter. Mr. Wen, however, would like to marry her himself. So he said to the aunt, " It's difficult to get an excellent son-in-law nowadays. What would you think about a man like me?" The aunt said, "We're in such dire straits, if my daughter could live a plain life, it would comfort me enough. How dare I expect a man like you?"

After a few days, Mr. Wen told his aunt: "I've already found a man for your daughter. His family status is not bad and he is in a good position. Everything he has can match mine." Then he held out a mirror stand made of jade as an engagement gift. The aunt was pleased.

When the wedding was over, the daughter put away her silk fan and laughed with a clap: "I guessed that it was you, my dear, and it was indeed as I expected."

Liu Yiqing (403-444)
Shi Shuo Xin Yu (New Accounts of Old Episodes)

33. 王戎宿慧

　　王戎七歲，嘗與諸小兒游。看道邊李樹多子折枝，諸兒競走取之，唯戎不動。人問之，答曰：“樹在道邊而多子，此必苦李。”取之信然 。

　　　　　　　　　　　　　　劉義慶《世說新語》

33. Clever Lad Wang Rong

When Wang Rong (234-305) was seven years old, once he was playing with other children, and they saw a plum tree by the road, which was so laden with fruit that its branches bent down close to the ground. All the children flocked around it to pick the plums except Wang Rong.

When asked why, he said, "The tree is just by the roadside, how come it remains so full of fruit. Its fruit must be bitter." The children stared at him in disbelief. But after tasting the fruit, they were convinced.

Liu Yiqing (403-444)
Shi Shuo Xin Yu (New Accounts of Old Episodes)

34. 劉晨阮肇

漢明帝永平五年 (62)，剡縣劉晨、阮肇共入天台山取榖皮，迷不得返。經十三日，糧食乏盡，飢餒殆死。遙望山上，有一桃樹，大有子實；而絕巖邃澗，永登無路。攀援藤葛，乃得至上。各啖數枚，而飢止體充。復下山，持杯取水，欲盥漱。見蕪菁葉從山腹流出，甚鮮新，復一杯流出，有胡麻飯糝。相謂曰：「此必去人徑不遠。」便共沒水，逆流二三里，得度山，出山一大溪。

溪邊有二女子，姿質妙絕，見二人持杯出，便笑曰：「劉阮二郎，捉向所失流杯來。」晨肇既不識之，緣二女便呼其姓，如似有舊，乃相見欣喜。問：「來何晚耶？」因邀還家。其家筒瓦屋。南壁及東壁下各有一大牀，皆施絳羅帳，帳角懸鈴，金銀交錯。牀頭各有十

34. Liu and Ruan in Fairyland

Five years after Emperor Ming (58-75) of the Han Dynasty came to the throne, Liu Chen and Ruan Zhao, from Shan County, made an excursion into the Tiantai Mountains to collect husks of rice. They lost their way home. Thirteen days had passed when they ran out of food and almost starved to death. Suddenly they saw a peach tree with large fruit on a hill in the distance, but a steep precipice and deep gully blocked the path towards it. By climbing up a creeper they finally reached the spot. Each of them ate a few peaches, and soon they were no longer hungry and regained their energy. Then they climbed down the hill. While they were scooping up water with cups to wash themselves, they saw some pieces of turnip leaves floating on the brook from the heart of the mountains. The leaves were pretty fresh. After a while a cup drifted out with sesame seeds and rice in it. The two men said to each other, "We can't be far away from civilisation!" They walked into the water together against the current for a few miles, and climbed up the mountain where before long they found a big stream.

By the stream there were two gorgeous girls. Seeing the two men coming forth with the cup in hand, the girls said with a smile, "Mr. Liu and Mr. Ruan, you're holding the cup we lost. It had drifted away." Liu and Ruan did not ever know the girls, but the girls called them by their names, as if they had known them for ages. So the men were overjoyed to see the girls. The girls asked, "Why have you taken such a long time to come here?"

They invited the men to their house made of bamboo tiles. By the south wall and the east wall stood two large beds surrounded by purple silk bed-curtains. The corners of the curtains were decorated with hanging bells. Gold and silver threads crisscrossed all

侍婢。敕云："劉阮二郎，經涉山岨，向雖得瓊實，猶尚虛弊，可速作食。"食胡麻飯、山羊脯、牛肉，甚甘美。食畢，行酒。有一羣女來，各持五三桃子，笑言："賀汝婿來。"酒酣作樂，劉阮欣怖交并。至暮，令各就一帳宿，女往就之，言聲清婉，令人忘憂。

十日後，欲求還去，女云："君己來是，宿福所牽，何復欲還耶？"遂停半年。氣候草木是春時，百鳥啼鳴，更懷悲思，求歸甚苦。女曰："罪牽君當可如何？"遂呼前來女子，有三四十人，集會奏樂，共送劉阮，指示還路。

既出，親舊零落，邑屋改異，無復相識。問訊得七世孫，傳聞上世入山，迷不得歸。至晉太元八年(383)，忽復去，不知何所。

劉義慶《幽明錄》

over the curtains. By each bed ten maids were standing. The two girls ordered them: "Mr.Liu and Mr. Ruan have travelled across mountains and rivers. Though they have eaten some peaches, they must still be very hungry and tired. Go and cook for then quickly." After a while, rice, goat meat and beef were served. The food was delicious.

After dinner, they drank, A group of girls came up with some peaches in their hands, and declared with a smile: "We congratulate you on the arrival of your husbands." Drinking to the full, Liu and Ruan both enjoyed themselves with the two girls. The two men felt both joy and fear. When night fell, each went to bed with one of the girls joining him. The voices of the girls were so gentle and soothing that the men left all their worries behind.

Ten days later, the men wanted to take leave, but the girls said, "You've only just arrived, and are having such a wonderful time. Why do you want to leave?" So the men remained for another half year. When spring came, and the birds were singing, the men were badly homesick. They begged to return home. The girls said, "Worldly thoughts draw you back to the world, there's no help for this." Then they called upon thirty to forty girls to play music, and bid farewell to Liu and Ruan, pointing out to them the way home.

As Liu and Ruan came out of the mountains, they failed to find any relatives and friends. Towns and houses all looked different, and there was nothing that they could recognize. After asking around, they found only their seventh generation of descendents, who had a legend that their ancestors went into the mountains, lost themselves and never came back.

One day in the eighth year of the Taiyuan period of the Jin Dynasty (383), the two suddenly left again, and no one had any idea where they had gone.

Liu Yiqing (403-444)
You Ming Lu (Tales of the Other World)

35. 賣胡粉女子

有人家甚富，止有一男，寵恣過常。游市，見一女子美麗，賣胡粉[1]，愛之，無由自達，乃託買粉，日往市，得粉便去，初無所言。積漸久，女深疑之。明日復來。問曰：「君買此粉，將欲何施？」答曰：「意相愛樂，不敢自達，然恆欲相見，故假此以觀姿耳。」女悵然有感，遂相許以私，剋以明夕。

其夜，安寢堂屋，以俟女來，薄暮果到。男不勝其悅，把臂曰：「宿願始伸於此！」歡踊遂死。女惶懼，不知所以，因遁去，明還粉店。至食時，父母怪男不起，往視，已死矣。

當就殯斂，發篋笥中，見百餘裹胡粉，大小一積。其母曰：「殺吾兒者，必此粉也。」入市遍買胡粉，次此女，比之手跡如先，遂執問女曰：「何殺吾兒？」女聞嗚咽，具以實陳。父母不信，遂以訴官。女曰：「妾

---

(1) 胡粉：搽臉的含鉛白粉。

35. The Girl Selling Face Powder

A well-off family had only one son. They doted upon him. Once while strolling around the market, the son saw a pretty girl selling face powder. He fell in love with her at once. However he had no chance to convey his adoration to her. He went to the market every day with the excuse of buying powder. As soon as the powder came to hand, he would take leave without saying a word. By and by the girl began to feel suspicious.

Next day when the son appeared again, she asked him, "What do you buy the powder for?" He replied, "I'm in love with you, however I dare not express it to you. But I'm always dying to see you, so I come to buy powder for the purpose of appreciating your beauty." The girl was moved by his sentimentality. They agreed to meet the next evening in privacy.

Next evening, the son lay in bed quietly, waiting for the girl. When dusk fell, she arrived. The son could not control his joy. He put his arms around the girl and said, "My long-cherished wish is finally realized!" That night he died of too much joy. The girl was so scared that she just found nowhere to go. At last she escaped back to the powder store at dawn.

It was already time for breakfast, but the son didn't get up. The parents became concerned, and went to his room, only to find him dead in bed.

Before carrying his body to the grave, the parents discovered inside a small suitcase many packets of powder. The mother said, "It must be this powder that killed my son!" Then they went throughout the market to find out the source of the powder. When they found the girl and saw the same kind of powder as that which their son had, they reproved her: "Why did you kill our son?" The girl sobbed and told them the truth. They simply didn't believe her, and took legal proceedings against her.

豈復吝死，乞一臨尸盡哀。"縣令許焉。徑往撫之慟
哭，曰："不幸致此，若死魂而靈，復何恨哉！"男豁
然更生，具說情狀。遂為夫婦，子孫繁茂。

劉義慶《幽明錄》

The girl said, "I don't mind death, but I request you to allow me to approach his body and express my sorrow." The county magistrate gave her permission. As soon as she approached the body and touched it, she started to wail and cried out, "What a misfortune! If only the soul could still live after the death of the body, then there would be no remorse in me at all." All at once the son regained consciousness, and described the whole situation. Finally they got married and had many descendants.

Liu Yiqing (403-444)
You Ming Lu (Tales of the Other World)

36. 魏武帝見匈奴使

　　魏武[1]將見匈奴使，自以形陋，不足懷遠國，使崔季珪代當坐，自捉刀立牀頭。事畢，令間諜問曰：“魏王何如？”使曰：“魏王雅望非常，然牀頭捉刀人，乃英雄也！”魏武聞之，馳殺此使。

　　　　　　　　　　　　　　　殷芸《殷芸小說》

---

(1) 魏武：曹操，漢丞相，封魏王，其子曹丕篡漢立魏後，追尊為
　　武帝。

36. The King of Wei Interviews the Envoy of Hun

King Wu (155-220) of the State of Wei was going to receive the envoy of Hun[1]. But he felt himself lacking in the qualities required to keep other countries in awe. So he had Cui Jigui take his place on the throne, while he himself stood to one side holding a sword. When the interview was over, the King sent a spy to ask the envoy, "How do you like our King?" The envoy replied, "The King looks exceptional. However, the man standing to one side and holding a sword is of superior stature!" As soon as the King heard that the envoy was smart to recognize him already, he had the envoy pursued and killed.

Yin Yun (471-536)
Yin Yun Xiao Shuo (Novelettes Collected by Yin Yun)

---

(1) Hun: see Note 2 on page 49.

37. 子路遇虎

　　孔子嘗游於山，使子路取水，逢虎於水所，與共
戰，攬尾得之，內懷中；取水還，問孔子曰：“上士殺
虎如之何？”子曰：“上士殺虎持虎頭。”又問曰：
“中士殺虎如之何？”子曰：“中士殺虎持虎耳。”又
問：“下士殺虎如之何？”子曰：“下士殺虎捉虎
尾。”子路出尾棄之。因恚孔子曰：“夫子知水所有
虎，使我取水，是欲我死。”乃懷石盤，欲中孔子。又
問：“上士殺人如之何？”子曰：“上士殺人使筆
端。”又問：“中士殺人如之何？”子曰：“中士殺人
用舌端。”又問：“下士殺人如之何？”子曰：“下士

37. Zilu Runs into a Tiger

Once Confucius (551-476 BC) was wandering with Zilu, one of his disciples, in the mountains. He sent Zilu to get some water. By the water Zilu ran into a tiger. He fought with the tiger and eventually defeated it by seizing its tail. He cut off the tail, put it in his bosom and took the water back. He asked Confucius, "How would a first-class gentleman kill a tiger?"

"He would catch its head," Confucius replied.

"How would a second-class gentleman kill a tiger?" Zilu asked further.

"He would hold its ears," Confucius replied.

"How would a third-rate gentleman kill a tiger?" he again asked.

"He would seize its tail," answered the Master.

Zilu took out the tail and threw it away. Then he declared with anger, "Sir, you surely must have known that there could be a tiger by the water, nevertheless you sent me to fetch water. Did you want to have me killed?" He held a stone tray in his bosom, and was ready to throw it at Confucius. Before he did that, he asked again, "How would the first-class gentleman kill a human being?"

"He would kill him with his pen," said Confucius.

"How would the second-class gentleman kill a human being?" Zilu asked again.

"He would with his tongue," said Confucius.

"How would the third-rate gentleman kill a human being?" he asked again.

"With a stone tray," Confucius replied.

殺人懷石盤。"子路出而棄之，於是心服。

殷芸《殷芸小説》

At this Zilu took out the tray and threw it away, as he was deeply convinced.

Yin Yun (471-531)
Yin Yun Xiao Shuo (Novelettes Collected by Yin Yun)

38. 陳元方

漢末陳太丘寔[1] 與友人期行，期日中，過期不至，太丘捨去。去後乃至。其子元方時年七歲，在門外戲。客問元方：“尊君在否？”答曰：“待君久不至，已去。”友人便怒曰：“非人哉！與人期行，相委而去！”元方曰：“君與家君期日中時，過中不來，則是無信；對子罵父，則是無禮。”友人慚，下車引之。元方遂入門不顧。

殷芸《殷芸小說》

---

(1) 陳寔，字仲弓，任太丘長，故稱。其子陳紀，字元方。

38. A Boy of Integrity

Chen Shi, a county magistrate in the last years of the Han Dynasty, once made an appointment, with a friend to set off together on a trip at noon. But the friend did not come on time, so Chen started off alone. After a while, the friend arrived only to find Chen's seven-year-old son, Yuanfang, playing outside the house. The friend asked Yuanfang, "Is your father in?" Yuanfang replied, "He'd waited for you for quite a while, but you didn't come, so he's gone by himself already."

" Bastard!" the man muttered angrily. "How could he make an appointment and break it just like that?"

Yuanfang retorted, "You had an appointment with my father and yet you're late: this shows you're not trustworthy. What's more: you pour abuse on a person in front of his son: this is impudence!"

The friend was ashamed to hear this. He descended from his carriage, intending to offer his apologies, but the boy had already turned his back on him and re-entered the house.

Yin Yun (471-531)
Yin Yun Xiao Shuo (Novelettes Collected by Yin Yun)

39. 甕夢

俗説：有貧人止能辦隻甕之資，夜宿甕中，心計曰："此甕賣之若干，其息已倍矣。我得倍息，遂可販二甕，自二甕而為四，所得倍息，其利無窮。"遂喜而舞，不覺甕破。

殷芸《殷芸小説》

39. The Dream in a Jar

A story goes thus: Once there was a poor man whose only property was a huge jar. Lying in the jar one night, he went off into a fancy: "If I sell this jar at a good price, I can get double income; if I gain double income, I can come by two jars, then by the same means I can make four jars from two. I reap double income each time likewise, and the profit will be endless!" While he was thinking of this, he got so excited that he began to dance for joy. Rather carelessly, he broke his jar into pieces.

Yin Yun (471-531)
Yin Yun Xiao Shuo (Novelettes Collected by Yin Yun)

40. 晏嬰[1]

齊晏嬰短小，使楚，楚為小門於大門側，乃延晏子。嬰不入，曰：“使狗國，狗門入，今臣使楚，不當從狗門入。”王曰：“齊無人耶？”對曰：“齊使賢者使賢王，不肖者使不肖王。嬰不肖，故使王耳。”王謂左右曰：“晏嬰辭辯，吾欲傷之。”坐定，縛一人來。王問何謂者。左右曰：“齊人坐盜。”王視晏曰：“齊人善盜乎？”對曰：“嬰聞橘生於江南，至江北為枳，枝葉相似，其實味且不同，水土異也。今此人生於齊，不解為盜，入楚則為盜，其實不同，水土使之然也。”王笑曰：“寡人反取病焉。”

侯白《啟顏錄》

---

(1) 晏嬰：春秋時齊景公的宰相。

40. Yan Ying's Wit

Yan Ying (?-500 BC), Prime Minister of the State of Qi, was short of stature. Once, he was sent on a diplomatic mission to the State of Chu. The King of Chu had a small gateway dug next to the big gate in the city wall for "greeting" Yan. But Yan refused to go in. He said, " Visiting the country of dogs, one enters through the doorway for dogs. Today I visit Chu, I should not go through the gateway for dogs." The King then asked, "Is there no other envoy in Qi besides you?"

"Qi sends smart men to smart kings, plain men to plain kings," replied Yan. "I'm plain, and thus sent to visit Your Majesty."

The King said to his attendants, "Yan Ying really has a way with words. I'll give him a good lesson."

When they sat down, a man, tied with a rope, was brought in. The King asked who he was. The attendants answered, "A thief from Qi."

The King eyed Yan and asked him, "Are the people in Qi thievish?"

Yan said, "I hear that the orange grows south of the Yangzi River, but after being transplanted to the north, it's called the trifoliate orange instead. The branches and leaves are all the same but the taste is different. It's caused by the difference in the water and soil. Now this man didn't steal when he lived in Qi. When he came to Chu, he became a thief: the different cases stem from the difference in environment."

"I must have been asking for it!" the King said to himself with a wry smile.

Hou Bai
Qi Yan Lu (A Collection of Jokes)

41. 敬德不詔

　　吏部尚書唐儉與太宗棋，爭道。上大怒，出為潭
州。蓄怒未泄，謂尉遲敬德[1]曰：“唐儉輕我，我欲殺
之，卿為我證驗有怨言指斥。”敬德唯唯。明日對仗，
敬德頓首曰：“臣實不聞。”頻問，確定不移。上怒，
碎玉玦於地，奮衣入。良久索食，引三品以上皆入宴，
上曰：“敬德今日利益者各有三：唐儉免枉死，朕免枉
殺，敬德免曲從，三利也；朕有恕過之美，儉有再生之
幸，敬德有忠直之譽，三益也。”賞敬德一千段，羣臣
皆呼萬歲。

張鷟《朝野僉載》

---

(1) 尉遲敬德：唐尉遲恭，字敬德。

41. A General Who Does Not Ingratiate Himself

The Minister of Personnel Tang Jian once played chess with the Emperor Tai Zong (598-649) of the Tang Dynasty, and they were both well matched. The Emperor became angry with him, and he was relegated to a lower post in Tan Zhou. However, the Emperor had not relieved his anger, and he intended to punish him further. He said to his General Yuchi Jingde (585-658), "I lost face in front of Tang Jian, I want to have him killed. You must provide evidence that he was conspiring to rub my name in the dirt." Yuchi Jingde nodded.

The next day Tang Jian was confronted with Yuchi Jingde in court. Yuchi bowed and said, "I have not heard of any such occurrence." After being asked several times, Yuchi insisted on his reply.

The Emperor was so enraged that he smashed a piece of precious jade and took his leave in a furious mood. After a long while, he invited officials of the third rank and above to banquet with him. The Emperor declared, "Today Jingde corrected three mistakes and committed three good deeds. Tang Jian is saved from an erroneous execution, I am saved from mistaken judgement, and Jingde is saved from wrong acquiescence—these are the three corrections. On the other hand, I win the good reputation for tolerance, Jian wins the chance to live on, and Jingde wins credit for his loyalty and frankness—these are the three good deeds." He awarded Yuchi Jingde with one thousand yards of silk, and all the officials present hailed, "Long Live Your Majesty!"

Zhang Cu
Chao Ye Qian Zai (Anecdotes of the Court and among Folks)

42. 鷂死懷中

太宗得鷂，絕俊異，私自臂之，望見鄭公[1]，乃藏於懷。公知之，遂前白事，因語古帝王逸豫，微語諷諫。語久，帝惜鷂且死，而素嚴敬徵，欲盡其言。徵語不時盡，鷂死懷中。

劉餗《隋唐嘉話》

---

(1) 鄭公：唐魏徵，封鄭國公。

42. The Death of a Sparrow Hawk

Once Emperor Taizong (598-649) of the Tang Dynasty had a sparrow hawk, which was outstandingly smart. One day, while putting the bird on his arm and playing with it, Taizong saw the Duke of Zheng (Wei Zheng, 580-643) coming over. He hid the bird in his bosom hurriedly. The Duke had caught sight of it. He came up and made a report to His Majesty. Then he described how the late emperors sapped their ambition with hobbies and an easy life as an admonition. They talked for quite a while, Taizong worried about the bird, but he revered Zheng and let him go through with his words. By the time the Duke finished, the sparrow hawk had already died in the Emperor's bosom.

Liu Su
Sui Tang Jia Hua (Good Records of the Sui & Tang Dynasties)

43. 身死而法不可改

　　徐大理有功，每見武后殺人，必據法廷爭。嘗與后反覆，辭色愈厲，后大怒，令拽出斬之，猶回顧曰：「臣身雖死，法終不可改。」至市臨刑得免，除名為庶人。如是再三，終不挫折，朝廷倚賴，至今猶懷之。

　　　　　　　　　　　　　　　劉餗《隋唐嘉話》

43. I Can Be Killed, But Never the Law

Xu Yougong (635-702) was a supreme judge of the Tang Dynasty. Whenever he heard that Empress Wu (626-708) had ordered somebody's execution, he would argue according to the law and plead with her in strong words and a stern voice. As a result of his constant interference, the Empress was infuriated, and ordered him to be dragged out and be put to death. As he was being dragged out he turned his head and shouted: " You can kill me, but you can never kill the law!"

After he arrived at the execution spot, an order was received that he had been pardoned from death, but was stripped of his royal position, to become one of the common people.

Xu never gave in, even though such events occurred repeatedly. In fact the Court relied on him, and he has been revered right up to this very day.

Liu Su
Sui Tang Jia Hua (Good Records of the Sui & Tang Dynasties)

44. 韋秀莊

開元中（713-741），滑州刺吏韋秀莊，暇日來城樓望黃河。樓中忽見一人，長三尺許，紫衣朱冠，通名參謁。韋秀莊知非人類，問是何神。答曰："即城隍之主。"又問何來，答云："黃河之神欲毀我城，以端河路。我固不許。尅後五日，大戰於河湄。恐力不禁，故來求救於使君爾。若得二千人，持弓弩物色相助，必當克捷。君之城也，惟君圖之。"秀莊許諾，神乃不見。

至其日，秀莊帥勁卒二千人登城。河中忽爾晦冥。須臾，有白氣直上十餘丈，樓上有青氣出，相縈繞。秀莊命弓弩亂射白氣，氣形漸小，至滅。唯青氣獨存，逶

44. Subduing the God of the Yellow River

During the Kai Yuan period (713-741) of the Tang Dynasty, the prefect of Hua Zhou, Wei Xiuzhuang, once climbed up the tower of the city wall to have a look at the Yellow River. In the tower he came across a dwarf only three feet tall, who wore a purple robe and a vermilion hat. He introduced himself to Wei. Wei thought he must be an immortal, and asked him which deity he was. The reply was, "I'm the Lord of Hell of this town." Then Wei asked him why he had come up to the tower. The dwarf replied, "The god of the Yellow River wants to destroy our town to change the course of the river. I certainly cannot agree to this. In five days' time we will fight it out beside the river, but I'm afraid I'm hardly strong enough for this contest, therefore I have come to request your help. If you send two thousand archers to support me, I'll be sure to defeat him. This town also belongs to you, so please think about it." Wei agreed to his request, and the Lord of Hell disappeared.

When the day of the battle came, Wei led two thousand strong soldiers onto the tower. Suddenly the river turned rough and dark, and before long a white spout shot up into the air to a height of a dozen zhang[1]. Simultaneously a gust of black smoke suddenly spun out from the tower, and entangled with the white spout. Wei ordered his archers to shoot at the white spout. It gradually dwindled until it vanished altogether. Only the black smoke remained,

---

(1) 1 *zhang*=10 feet

111

迤如雲峰之狀，還入樓中。初時，黃河俯近城之下，此
後漸退，至今五六里也。

戴孚《廣異記》

spinning like a cloud cluster as it flew back into the tower.

In former times the river was at the foot of the city wall, but after this event, the river receded bit by bit. Nowadays the river is five or six *li* [2] away from the town.

Dai Fu
Guang Yi Ji (A Wide Collection of Oddities)

---

(2) 1 *li*=1/2 km

45. 童區寄傳

　　童寄者，郴州蕘牧兒也，行牧且蕘，二豪賊劫持反接，布囊其口，去逾四十里之虛所賣之。寄偽兒啼，恐慄為兒恆狀，賊易之，對飲，酒醉。一人去為市，一人臥，植刃道上。童微伺其睡，以縛背刃，力下上，得絕。因取刃殺之。逃未及遠，市者還，得童大駭，將殺童。遽曰："為兩郎僮，孰若為一郎童耶？彼不我恩也，郎誠見完與恩，無所不可。"市者良久計曰：與其殺是僮，孰若賣之，與其賣而分，孰若吾得專焉，幸而殺彼甚善。即藏其尸，持童抵主人所，愈束縛甚牢。夜半，童自轉以縛即爐火燒絕之。雖瘡手勿憚，復取刃殺

45. The Story of a Brave and Clever Boy

There was a lad called Ou Ji, who was a herdsboy and grasscutter. One day, while he was grazing his cattle and gathering grass, two bandits kidnapped him. They tied his hands behind his back with a rope and stuffed his mouth with a rag. They took him to a fair forty miles away to sell him.

Ou Ji pretended to blubber and shiver as ordinary children in fear do. So the bandits were off their guard. They enjoyed themselves in liquor and got drunk. Then one headed for the fair on business while the other slept with his sword standing by him on the road. Having waited till he was asleep, the lad turned his back towards the sword and began to rub the rope against the blade. He got free at last, and seized the sword and killed the sleeping bandit.

The lad hadn't escaped far before the other bandit came back from the fair. This bandit was shocked at what had happened.

When he caught the lad, he was about to kill him, but the lad said immediately, "For your sake, it is much better for me to serve you alone than to serve you both, wouldn't you think so? He didn't treat me well. If you don't kill me, and are kind to me, I won't mind doing anything for you!"

The bandit thought it over for some time: "It seems better to sell him than to kill him, and better to get all the money for myself than to share it with others. Fortunately, the lad has killed him." Then he buried the dead bandit and took the lad to the house of a buyer. He bound the lad more tightly.

In the middle of the night the lad moved close to the stove fire to burn up the rope. Though his hands were singed, he wasn't scared. When he freed himself at last, he killed the other bandit

市者，因大號，一虛皆驚。童曰：「我區氏兒也，不當
為僮，賊二人得我，我幸殺之矣，願以聞於官。」虛吏
白州，州白大府，大府召視兒幼愿耳，刺史顏證奇之，
留為小吏，不肯。與衣裳，吏護還之鄉。鄉之行劫縛
者，側目莫敢過其門。皆曰：「是兒少秦武陽二歲，而
討殺二豪，豈可近耶！」

柳宗元《柳河東集》

with the sword, then yelled loudly so that all the people in the fair were woken up. The lad declared, "I'm the son of the family Ou, not a boy servant. These two bandits kidnapped me. To my luck, I killed them. I'm willing to go to court." The headman of the fair reported the case to the prefect, the prefect reported it to the governor, who tried Ou Ji, only to find him a young lad. Prefect Yan Zheng wondered at him, and liked to keep the lad as his servant, but the lad had no interest in it. So Yan gave him some clothes and sent a servant to escort him home.

Since then kidnappers in his home village looked askance at the lad with fear and dare not pass by his house. They said, "He is two years younger than Qin Wuyang[1], but he has already killed two bandits in revenge. How could we have the guts to approach him?"

Liu Zongyuan (773-819)
Liu He Dong Ji (Collected Works of Liu Zongyuan)

---

(1) Qin Wuyang, living in the Warring States Period (475-221 BC) , was only 13 years old when he followed Jing Ke, of the State of Yan, to assassinate Qin Shihuang (Shih Huang-ti).

46. 兗公答參軍

陸兗公[1]為同州刺史,有家僮遇參軍不下馬。參軍怒,欲賈其事,鞭背見血。入白兗公,曰:"卑吏犯公,請去官。"公從容謂曰:"奴見官人不下馬,打也得,不打也得。官人打了,去也得,不去也得。"參軍不測而退。

李肇《國史補》

---

(1) 唐陸象先,封兗國公。

46. Duke Yan's Reply

Governor Lu (665-736) who was later made the Duke of Yan, assumed the post in Tongzhou. Once one of his servants did not descend from his horse as a sign of respect when he ran into a staff officer. The officer cut up rough, and whipped him on the back until blood came out.

After a while, the officer went to report to Governor Lu, apologising, "Your humble officer offended you by whipping your servant, please dismiss me from my post." Lu answered unhurriedly: "My servant met you, but didn't get off the horse, beating him or not is all the same. Now that you have beaten him, dismissing you or not is all the same too." The officer took leave, embarrassed by Lu's unexpected remark.

Li Zhao
Guo Shi Bu (Supplement to the History of the Tang Dynasty)

47. 王鍔散貨財

　　王鍔[1] 累任大鎮[2]，財貨山積。有舊客誡鍔以積而能散之義。後數日，客復見鍔。鍔曰：“前所見教，誠如公言·已大散矣。”客曰：“請問其目。”鍔曰：“諸男各與萬貫，女婿各與千貫矣。”

　　　　　　　　　　　　　　　　李肇《國史補》

---

(1) 王鍔：唐德宗在位時（780-783）為相，出身行伍，貪鄙好貨利。
(2) 鎮：方鎮。唐制設節度使統一管一道或數州軍、民、財政，號方鎮；簡稱鎮。

120

47. Wang E Distributes His Fortune

Since Wang E had held a high position of district governor for several times, he made a good fortune. An old guest of his warned him that he should not only hoard up fortune, but also share it out.

A few days later, the guest met Wang E again. Wang said, "I took your advice. Most of my fortune has already been distributed."

The guest asked, "Could you please go into the details?"

"I gave each son ten thousand *guan*[1], and each son-in-law one thousand."

Li Zhao
Guo Shi Bu (Supplement to the History of the Tang Dynasty)

---

(1)1 *guan*=1,000 coppers.

48. 文德皇后⁽¹⁾

　　太宗嘗罷朝，自言：「殺卻此田舍漢！」文德皇后
問：「誰觸忤陛下？」太宗曰：「魏徵⁽²⁾每庭辱我，使
我常不得自由。」皇后退，朝服立於庭。太宗驚曰：
「何為若是？」對曰：「妾聞主聖臣忠。今陛下聖明，
故魏徵得盡直言。妾備後宮，焉敢不賀！」於是太宗意
乃釋。

劉肅《大唐新語》

---

(1) 文德皇后：唐太宗的皇后長孫氏，謚文德。
(2) 魏徵：唐開國功臣，封鄭國公。

48. An Empress of Virtue

On returning from the imperial court, the Emperor, Tai Zong (598-649) of the Tang Dynasty murmured to himself, "I'll definitely kill this bumpkin!"

Empress Wen De (601-636) asked him, "Who offended Your Majesty?" Tai Zong replied, "Wei Zheng (580-643)[1]. He often dishonours me at court and makes me feel impeded in many ways."

The empress took leave after she heard this. Later she appeared at the gate of the palace in official dress. Tai Zong was surprised, saying, "What's all this show for?"

The empress answered, "I hear that the subjects of a state will be loyal only if the emperor is wise. Today Your Majesty is wise, so Wei Zheng wishes to act loyally and honestly. As your wife, how could I not congratulate you?"

The emperor felt better after hearing this.

Liu Su
Da Tang Xin Yu (New Accounts of the Tang Dynasty)

---

(1) Wei Zheng: Emperor Tai Zong's counsellor

49. 狂夫之言聖人擇焉

　　皇甫德參上書曰：“陛下修洛陽宮，是勞人也；收地租，是厚斂也；俗尚高髻，是宮中所化也。”太宗怒曰：“此人欲使國家不收一租，不役一人，宮人無髮，乃稱其意！”魏徵進曰：“賈誼當漢文之時上書云：‘可為痛哭者三，可為長嘆者五。’自古上書，率多激切；若非激切，則不能服人主之心。激切即似訕謗。所謂‘狂夫之言，聖人擇焉。’惟在陛下裁察，不可責之，否則於後誰敢言者？”乃賜絹二十疋，命歸。

　　　　　　　　　　　　　　劉肅《大唐新語》

49. Sages Attend to Ravings

Huangpu Decan submitted a statement to Emperor Tai Zong (598-649): "Your Majesty, it is a waste of manpower to build the palace at Luoyang, and it is exploitation to demand land rent. People follow the fashion to coil up the hair just because it is the style in the imperial palace." Tai Zong was annoyed, saying, " This fellow wants the government to levy no rent and exact no one's labour, and he wants the people in the palace to have no hair. Then he will be pleased."

Wei Zheng (580-643)[1] said, "Jia Yi (201-169 BC) submitted a statement in the time of Emperor Wen (179-157 BC) of the Han Dynasty, saying, 'Here are three cases to cry over, and five cases to sigh about.' Since the old times, the statements to the emperors have been sharp but sincere. If not so, how could one ever move the emperor to make a decision? These sharp words may sound wild and slanderous. That is why they say, 'Sages attend to ravings'! I implore Your Majesty to think about this, and not to rebuke the writer. Otherwise who would dare to advise you in the future?"

Then the Emperor rewarded Huangpu twenty rolls of silk and let him return home.

Liu Su
Da Tang Xin Yu (New Accounts of the Tang Dynasty)

---

(1) Wei Zheng: see footnote on p123.

50. 旗亭賭唱

　　開元中，詩人王昌齡、高適、王之渙齊名。時風塵未偶，而游處略同。一日天寒微雪，三詩人共詣旗亭，貰酒小飲。忽有梨園伶官數十人，登樓會讌。三詩人因避席隈映，擁爐火以觀焉。俄有妙妓四輩，尋續而至，奢華艷曳，都冶頗極。旋則奏樂，皆當時之名部也。昌齡等私相約曰："我輩各擅詩名，每不自定其甲乙，今者可以密觀諸伶所謳，若詩入歌詞之多者，則為優矣。"俄而一伶拊節而唱，乃曰："寒雨連江夜入吳，平明送客楚山孤。洛陽親友如相問，一片冰心在玉壺。"昌齡則引手畫壁曰："一絕句。"尋又一伶謳之

50. A Wager on Songs

There were three poets in the period of Kai Yuan (713-741) of the Tang Dynasty, Wang Changling, Gao Shi and Wang Zhihuan, who were equally famous. They were subject to much the same experiences and griefs in their early years.

One day, as it was cold and snowing lightly, the three poets visited a wine house to have a drink. After a while, several tens of the actors and actresses of the imperial theatre also arrived to hold a party upstairs. The poets got up to offer seats to them and found seats in a place next to the fire. Soon four pretty female singers came in one by one. The girls were all extravagantly dressed and beautifully made up for the occasion. In a short time they began performing the popular tunes of the period.

The poets discussed among themselves, " We are reputed for writing poems but we don't know who excels. Let's agree that whichever one of us has more poems turned into songs by the singers is most certainly the best known. Let us listen to their singing to decide this matter."

The first girl began her song as follows: "Cold rain fell over the river running down to Wu the previous night. In the twilight I saw you off, feeling as lonely as Mount Chu. At Luoyang, should you meet my friends and relatives who ask after me, please tell them my heart is as pure as an ice crystal in a jade pot."

Changling stretched out his arm and made a mark on the wall: "One poem by me."

曰：“開篋淚霑臆，見君前日書。夜臺[1]何寂寞，猶是子雲[2]居。”適則引手畫壁曰：“一絕句。”尋又一伶謳曰：“奉帚平明金殿開，強將團扇共徘徊。玉顏不及寒鴉色，猶帶昭陽日影來。”昌齡則又引手畫壁曰：“二絕句。”之渙自以得名已久，因謂諸人曰：“此輩皆潦倒樂官，所唱皆巴人下俚之詞耳，豈陽春白雪之曲，俗物敢近哉！”因指諸妓之中最佳者曰：“待此子所唱，如非我詩，吾即終身不敢與子爭衡矣。脫是吾詩，子等當須列拜牀下，奉吾為師。”因歡笑而俟之。須臾，次至雙鬟發聲，則曰：“黃沙遠上白雲間，一片孤城萬仞山。羌笛何須怨楊柳，春風不度玉門關。”之渙即摭歈二子曰：“田舍奴，我豈妄哉？”因大諧笑。

---

(1) 夜臺：墳墓。
(2) 子雲：揚雄字，西漢末年著名學者。

The second girl began her song as follows: "My chest was wet with tears, as I opened the suitcase and found your old letters. Lonely is the tomb in which you rest, like Yang Ziyun's[1] home in solitude."

Gao Shi stretched out his arm and made his mark on the wall: "One by me."

The third girl began her song: "At dawn I swept the ground as the palace gates opened; with a fan in hand, I lingered around and pondered: Why does my face look pale before the crows which still carry the sunny shadow of the palace?"

At this Changling declared, "Another of mine!"

Zhihuan, regarding himself as having become famous for a long time, retorted against the other two, "Such common girls singing such common songs. How can we expect such wenches to sing the words of the true poet?" At this he pointed to the most beautiful of the girls and said, "Wait to hear what she sings. I am sure she will be singing one of my poems. If not I shall never rival with either of you again. But if she does you must both bow down before me and call me master." They all laughed together and waited to see what the girl would sing.

The girl, with her hair coiled up on both sides of her head, began her song: "A vast expanse of yellow sand reaches up the distant white clouds. Here stands a lonely town amongst the lofty mountains. In vain the tones of the Qiang flute lament the late budding of the willows. For the spring breezes could never cross the Yu Men Pass."

"Bumpkins!" Zhihuan responded in satisfaction. "Was I not right after all?" The three of them all roared with laughter, which

---

(1) Yang Ziyun: alias Yang Xiong, an eminent scholar of the late Western Han Dynasty (205 BC- 8 AD).

諸伶不喻其故，皆起詣曰：「不知諸郎君何此歡噱？」
昌齡等因話其事。諸伶競拜曰：「俗眼不識神仙，乞降
清重，俯就筵席。」三子從之，飲醉竟日。

薛用弱《集異記》

attracted the attention of the girls, who came over to ask what had made them so merry suddenly.

Changling told them what happened, and the girls bowed to them in respect, saying, "Pardon us common girls for not recognizing you as such great poets. Please grant us the honour of being guests at our party."

The poets accepted the invitation and made merry the whole day long.

Xue Yongruo
Ji Yi Ji (A Collection of Anecdotes)

51. 武則天讀檄

　　駱賓王為徐敬業作檄，極疏大周[1]過惡。則天覽及
"蛾眉不肯讓人，狐媚偏能惑主"，微笑而已。至"一
抔之土未乾，六尺之孤安在"，不悦曰："宰相何得失
如此人！"

　　　　　　　　　　　　　　　段成式《酉陽雜俎》

---

(1) 大周：武則天稱帝，國號曰周。

51. Wu Zetian[1] Reading the Proclamation against Herself

Luo Binwang (?-684) drew up a proclamation for General Xu Jinye against the Empress Wu Zetian (626-708) who usurped the rule of the Tang Dynasty. She read the proclamation against her, which was as follows: "A beautiful woman, she grasped every opportunity of advancement, and using her charms, this vixen bewitched the Emperor." At this a slight smile crossed her face. As she read on she came across a further blight to her character: "Alas, where is the Crown Prince when the earth on the Emperor's grave is not yet set?" She reacted with displeasure, "How could the Prime Minister ignore this man?"[2]

Duan Chengshi (?-863)
You Yang Za Zu (You Yang Records of Myriad Things)

---

(1) Wu Zetian usurped the throne between 690-705 during the Tang Dynasty and was the first woman emperor and dictator in Chinese history.
(2) Wu Zetian, contrary to expectation, was not angry about the censure on her but was displeased because the Prime Minister did not recommend to her Luo Bingwang who wrote the moving lines showing his learning and literary talent.

52. 王勃展才

　　王勃著滕王閣序，時年十四。都督閻公不之信，勃雖在座，而閻公意屬子婿孟學士為之，已宿構矣。及以紙筆巡讓賓客，勃不辭讓。公大怒，拂衣而起；專令人伺其下筆。第一報云：“南昌故郡，洪都新府；”公曰：“亦是老生常談！”又報云：“星分翼軫，地接衡廬。”公聞之，沈吟不言。又云：“落霞與孤鶩齊飛，秋水共長天一色。”公矍然而起曰：“此真天才，當垂不朽矣！”遂亟請宴所，極歡而罷。

王定保《唐摭言》

52. Wang Bo Displays His Talent

When Wang Bo (648-675) wrote his masterpiece "Ode to the Tower of Prince Teng", he was only fourteen years old. Knowing little about him, the prefect of Hongzhou, whose name was Yan, did not recognize the lad's talent. Although he had invited Wang to the celebration for the rebuilding of the tower, he asked his son-in-law, a scholar called Meng, to write for the occasion a composition which in fact was prepared beforehand.

When all the guests had assembled for the event, they were invited (as a matter of courtesy) to prepare a composition, and only Wang accepted. Yan was furious. He rose, and told a servant to watch what Wang was writing and report to him immediately. The first sentence came to his ears: "This tower in the former capital, Nanchang, is now the new centre of Hongzhou." There was nothing new in this, he thought.

The second sentence arrived: "In the sky, right above this place, are the stars Yi and Zhen; On the earth, this spot is connected with the famous mountains Heng and Lu." This couplet moved Yan to silent thought.

The third sentence soon reached his ears: "The evening clouds drift with a solitary goose in company, and the hue of the autumn river blends with that of the endless sky." On hearing this, Yan jumped up, shouting: "What a talent! This couplet will be remembered for ever!"

Hurriedly he invited Wang Po to have dinner together, and they had a wonderful time.

Wang Dingbao
Tang Zhi Yan (Anecdotes of the Tang Dynasty)

53. 掘地皮

　　徐知訓[1] 在宣州，聚斂苛暴，百姓苦之。入覲侍宴，伶人戲作綠衣大面，若鬼神者。傍一人問：“誰何？”對曰：“我宣州土地神也，吾主入覲，和地皮掘來，故得至此。”

　　　　　　　　　　　鄭文寶《江南餘載》

---

(1) 徐知訓：唐末十國吳相徐溫之子。

53. Peel Off the Earth

Xu Zhixun (?-918), magistrate of Xuanzhou, was a ruthless despot oppressing the people and extorting money from them wilfully. Once he went to court and attended the imperial banquet. On the stage appeared a performer who was dressed in a green robe and wore a demon mask. Another performer then asked him, "Where do you come from and what is your position?" The reply was, "I used to be the earth deity of Xuanzhou, but the magistrate came to court and brought the earth peeled off with him, so I am here."

Zheng Wenbao (953-1013)
Jiang Nan Yu Zai (Stories of the South)

54. 奈何縱民稼穡

　　莊宗[1]好田獵，獵於中牟，踐民田。中牟縣令當馬切諫，為民請。莊宗怒，叱縣令去，將殺之。伶人敬新磨知其不可，乃率諸伶走追縣令，擒至馬前，責之曰：「汝為縣令，獨不知吾天子好獵耶？奈何縱民稼穡，以供稅賦？何不飢汝縣民，而空此地，以備吾天子之馳騁？汝罪當死！」因前，請亟行刑。諸伶共倡和之。莊宗大笑，縣令乃得免去。

　　　　　　　　　　　　　歐陽修《新五代史》

---

(1) 莊宗：李存勗，唐末繼梁建國，號曰唐。

54. Why Have the Field Cultivated

Emperor Zhuang Zong of the Hou Tang Dynasty (923-936) loved hunting. Once while he went hunting in Zhongmu, he rode straight through a field under cultivation. The prefect of Zhongmu stopped the Emperor's horse and, admonishing him in an earnest tone, pleaded with him for the sake of the peasants. Becoming irritated at this, Zhuang Zong bawled at the prefect and intended to have him killed.

There was an actor, by the name of Jing Xinmo, who having heard of the incident, felt that it was unfair. Leading a group of other actors he intercepted the prefect and brought him before the Emperor.

The actor scolded the prefect, saying, "You are the prefect, and yet you don't know His Majesty loves hunting. Why do you allow the peasants to cultivate the fields to earn tax? Why not starve them in order for the field to remain empty for His Majesty to gallop on? You certainly are committing a capital crime!"

After he said this, he requested for the immediate execution of the prefect while the other actors chanted along with him. Zhuang Zong was so amused that he laughed and granted the pardon of the prefect.

Ouyang Xiu(1007-1072)
Xin Wu Dai Shi (A New History of the Five Dynasties)

55. 賣油翁

　　陳康肅公[1] 善射，當世無雙，公亦以此自矜。嘗射於家圃，有賣油翁釋擔而立，睨之久而不去。見其發矢十中八、九，但微頷之。康肅問曰：“汝亦知射乎？”翁曰：“無他，但手熟爾。”康肅忿然曰：“爾安敢輕吾射！”翁曰：“以我酌油知之。”乃取一葫盧[2] 置於地，以錢覆其口，徐以杓酌油瀝之，自錢孔入而錢不濕，因曰：“我亦無他，惟手熟爾。”康肅笑而遣之。

歐陽修《歸田錄》

---

(1) 陳康肅公：名堯咨，謚康肅。
(2) 葫盧：即以葫蘆為盛器。

55. An Old Oil Pedlar

During the Song Dynasty there was an official, named Chen
Yaozi, who was extremely proud of his matchless skill of archery.
One day as he was practising in his courtyard, an old oil pedlar
passing by put down his shoulder pole and load, and stood regard-
ing the archer for a long period of time. He nodded each time as
Chen's arrows hit the target eight to nine times out of ten.

Chen, noticing the pedlar, spoke out to him, "Do you also
know about archery? Am I not a good shot?"

"It seems that you practise much, but nothing more than that,"
answered the old man.

Chen, angered by this, shouted back at him, "How dare you
belittle my skill!"

The old man responded with an explanation: "I know this to be
true through my experience of pouring oil." He placed a gourd on
the ground, and on the opening at the top of the gourd, he placed a
coin with a square hole in its centre. He filled his ladle and began
to slowly pour its contents through the hole in the coin. The oil
flowed through smoothly, without even wetting the coin. After he
had finished, he spoke again, "I have achieved this through practice, and with you it's the same."

Chen smiled after he saw this demonstration, and let the man
go.

Ouyang Xiu (1007-1072)
Gui Tian Lu (Notes Written in the Years of Retirement)

56. 靴價

　　馮相道、和相凝[1]，同在中書。一日，和問馮曰：
"公靴新買，其值幾何？"馮舉左足示和，曰："九
佰。"和性褊急，遽回顧小吏，云："吾靴何得用一千
八佰？"因詬責。久之，馮徐舉其右足曰："此亦九
佰。"於是哄堂大笑。

　　　　　　　　　　　　　歐陽修《歸田錄》

---

(1) 馮道、和凝：五代時人，道歷事四姓十君，後晉天福二年（937）
　　以司空兼門下侍郎，同中書門下平章事；凝於後晉天福五年
　　（940）以翰林學士承旨、戶部侍郎為中書侍郎，同中書門下平
　　章事。

56. The Price of Boots

There were once two chancellors called Feng Dao (882-954) and He Ning (898-955) who worked together in the government secretariat. One day He Ning noticed that Feng Dao was wearing new boots, and he asked him how much they had cost him. Feng held up his left foot and said, "Nine hundred coppers." His associate was an impatient man. He turned and glared at his petty official, blaming and scolding: "How come mine cost one thousand eight hundred?" After a good while, Feng Dao held up his right foot and said, "This one also cost nine hundred." At this the whole office was reduced to laughter.

Ouyang Xiu (1007-1072)
Gui Tian Lu (Notes Written in the Years of Retirement)

57. 傍鑿一池

往年，士大夫好講水利，有言欲涸梁山泊以為農田，或詰之曰："梁山泊古鉅野澤，廣袤數百里，今若涸之，不幸秋夏之交，行潦四集，諸水并入，何以受之？"貢父⁽¹⁾適在座，徐曰："卻於泊之傍鑿一池，大小正同，則可受其水矣。"座中皆絕倒，言者大慚沮。

王闢之《澠水燕談錄》

---

(1) 貢父：宋劉攽字。

144

57. To Make Another Pool

Once upon a time there were some scholars discussing the matter of water conservancy. One suggested draining off the water of the Liang Shan Lake to till the land. The others asked, "Liang Shan Lake is a natural water reserve of ancient times. It occupies several hundred miles. If it's drained, where will the water from the autumn floods be stored when it pours in from all directions?"

Liu Gongfu (1023-1089)[1], who happened to be there also, said assuredly, "Just make another pool of the same size nearby to hold the water." The others doubled up with laughter, and the speaker was extremely embarrassed.

Wang Pizhi (1023-?)
Mian Shui Yan Tan Lu (Records of Chats on Mian Shui)

---

(1) Liu Gongfu: a historian of the Northern Song Dynasty (960-1127) in Chinese history.

58. 小名和尚

　　歐陽文忠[1] 不喜釋氏，有談佛者，必正色視之；而公之幼子小字和尚，或問：“公既不喜佛，排浮屠，而以和尚名子，何也？”公曰：“所以賤之也。如今人家以牛、驢名小兒耳。”問者大笑，且伏公之辯也。

　　　　　　　　　　　王闢之《澠水燕談錄》

---

(1) 宋歐陽修，謚文忠。

58. Pet Name

Ouyang Wenzhong (1007-1072)[1] disliked Buddhism, and whenever others talked about it, he would glare at them. His youngest son's pet name was Monk, and others often asked, "If you don't care about Buddhism and object to it so much, why do you call your son Monk?"

His reply was: "It's the way I look down upon Buddhism. I use the name 'Monk' for my child just as others call their children by the names of 'Ox' or 'Donkey'." Everybody laughed and was convinced by his logic.

Wang Pizhi (1023-?)
Mian Shui Yan Tun Lu (Records of Chats on Mian Shui)

---

(1) Ouyang Wenzhong: better known as Ouyang Xiu, was the famous poet, writer, historian and politician of the Song Dynasty (960-1279) in Chinese history.

59. 晏元獻

　　晏元獻公⁽¹⁾ 為童子⁽²⁾ 時，張文節⁽³⁾ 薦之於朝廷，召至闕下，適值御試進士，便令公就試。公一見試題，曰：“臣十日前已作此賦，有賦草尚在，乞別命題。”上極愛其不隱。及為館職，時天下無事，許臣寮擇勝燕飲，當時侍從文館士大夫各為燕集，以至市樓酒肆，往往皆供帳為遊息之地。公是時甚貧，不能出，獨家居與昆弟講習。一日選東宮官，忽自中批除晏殊。執政莫諭所因，次日進覆，上諭之曰：“近聞館閣臣寮，無不嬉遊燕賞，彌日繼夕，唯殊杜門與兄弟讀書，如此謹厚，正可為東宮官。”公既受命，得對，上面諭除授之意，公語言質野，則曰：“臣非不樂燕遊者，直以貧無可為

---

(1) 晏元獻公：晏殊，謚元獻，仁宗朝累官至同中書門下平章事。
(2) 童子：《宋史 • 選舉志》：凡童子十五歲以下，能通經作詩賦，州升諸朝，而天子親試，其命官免舉無常格。
(3) 張文節：張知白，謚文節，真宗時參贊大政。

59. Yan Shu's Honesty

Yan Shu (991-1055) was below fifteen when he was recommended by Zhang Wenjie for summoning to the court. At that time, the imperial examinations were being held, and the Emperor ordered Yan Shu to attend an examination with the rest of the scholars. As soon as he saw the title of the essay that was to be written, Yan Shu said to the Emperor, "Ten days ago I wrote an essay with this very same title and I have the manuscript on hand. Would it not be better to assign another subject for my examination?" The Emperor was impressed by his honesty.

When he was working for the Imperial Academy in peace time, the courtiers and officials were allowed to have banquets. Those working in the academies would often also hold parties, and as a result the restaurants, tea-shops and inns often became the favourite haunts of such people. At that time Yan lived a poor life, and he could not afford to party with his associates, but stayed at home to study instead with his brothers.

One day, an occasion for selecting an official to serve the prince in the Eastern Palace arose, and surprisingly, the Emperor nominated Yan Shu for the post. The Prime Minister and other important court officials could not understand the decision. The next day, as they attended court, the Emperor declared, "Recently I have heard that the officials and academics all enjoy themselves on trips and in banquets, partying from dawn till night. Only Yan Zhu stays at home and studies with his brothers. Such a prudent man is fit to become an official in the Eastern Palace."

After his appointment, as was the custom, Yan Shu entered the palace to be received by the Emperor. When he heard of the reasons why he was appointed, he stated to the Emperor frankly, "I also like to have parties and trips in scenic spots, only that I cannot afford to do so as I am a poor man. If I had money, I would also go

之具。臣若有錢，亦須往，但無錢不能出耳。”上益嘉
其誠實，知事君體，眷注日深。仁宗朝，卒至大用。

沈括《夢溪筆談》

out." The Emperor praised his honesty and his faithfulness to the court, and trusted him more and more. When the prince became Emperor, Yan Shu was appointed Prime Minister.

Shen Kuo (1029-1093)
Meng Xi Bi Tan (Sketches on Dream Brook)

60. 乘隙

濠州定遠縣一弓手，善用矛，遠近皆服其能。有一偷亦善擊刺，常蔑視官軍，唯與此弓手不相下。曰：「見必與之決生死。」一日弓手者因事至村步，適值偷在市飲酒，勢不可避，遂曳矛而鬭。觀者如堵牆。久之，各未能進。弓手者忽謂偷曰：「尉至矣，我與汝皆健者，汝敢與我尉馬前決生死乎？」偷曰：「諾。」弓手應聲刺之，一舉而斃，蓋乘其隙也。

又有人曾遇強寇鬭。矛刃方接，寇先含水滿口，忽噀其面，其人愕然，刃已揕胸。後有一壯士，復與寇遇，已先知噀水之事，寇復用之。水纔出口，矛已洞頸。蓋已陳芻狗，其機已失，恃勝失備，反受其害。

沈括《夢溪筆談》

60. Exploiting an Oversight

There was an archer of Dingyuan, Haozhou, who was skilful with the spear and was admired by folks from far and near. There was also a thief skilful at thrusting, who looked down upon all official militiamen, except for this archer. Once the thief declared, "If I ever meet him, I will certainly challenge him to a duel."

One day the archer came over to a village on business, and the thief happened to be drinking in the market. So, a fight was inevitable. As they fought with spears, a big crowd of spectators gathered around them. After a while neither of them managed to get the better of the other. All at once the archer said to the thief, "An official is coming. You and I are equally strong, do you have the guts to fight it out with me in front of him?" The thief replied, "Sure." No sooner had he spoken than the archer thrust his spear into him, immediately killing him. The archer exploited the oversight of his opponent.

There was also another man who ran into a highwayman. They fought against each other with sword and spear. The highwayman kept his mouth full of water, and suddenly spat the water in the other's face. The man was stunned, and the same moment he thrust his sword into the man's chest. Later a warrior, having heard about this highwayman's trick, met him. The highwayman played exactly the same trick again. But this time as soon as the water was spat out, the spear of the warrior had already made a hole in his throat.

The above reminds us of the sacrificial straw dog which, after being put to ceremonial use once, is on longer useful. Setting all mind on past victories won by deceit and being off his guard, man will see his defeat thereby.

Shen Kuo (1029-1093)
Meng Xi Bi Tan (Sketches on Dream Brook)

61. 劉沈處世

　　《南史》：劉凝之為人認所著履，即與之。此人後得所失履，送還，不肯復取。又沈驎士亦為鄰人認所著履，驎士笑曰：「是卿履耶？」即與之。鄰人得所失履，送還，驎士曰：「非卿履耶？」笑而受之。此雖小事，然處世當如驎士，不當如凝之也。

蘇軾《志林》

61. Different Attitudes to Others' Mistakes

The *History of the Southern Dynasties* recorded an anecdote involving Liu Ningzhi (390-448). Somebody had mistaken Liu's shoes for his own, and Liu gave the shoes to him. Later that person found his own shoes, and sent Liu's shoes back to him, but Liu did not accept the returned shoes.

A similar event occurred to Shen Linshi (419-503). Shen's neighbour took his shoes by mistake. Shen smiled saying, "Are they yours?" and gave the shoes to him. Soon the neighbour found the shoes he had lost and sent Shen's shoes back. Shen asked if they weren't really his neighbour's, then smiled and took them back.

These are trivial matters, but it would be better for us to act rather as Shen than as Liu.

Su Shi (1036-1101)
Zhi Lin (Short Essays)

62. 措大喫飯

　　有二措大相與言志。一云：“我平生不足，惟飯與睡耳。他日得志，當喫飽飯了便睡，睡了又喫飯。”一云：“我則異於是。當喫了又喫，何暇復睡耶？”吾來廬山，聞馬道士善睡，於睡中得妙。然吾觀之，終不如彼措大得喫飯三昧也。

　　　　　　　　　　　　　蘇軾《志林》

156

62. Two Shabby Pedants Chat about Eating

Two shabby pedants chatted about their ambitions. One said, "In my life, all I'm short of are food and sleep. When I become rich, I'll sleep after eating and eat after sleeping." The other said, "I won't be like you. I'll eat and eat, with little time to think of sleep!"

When I was in Lushan, I heard of Taoist Ma, who was addicted to sleeping and enjoyed himself in sleep. But as I see it, I don't think his enjoyment in sleep can compare with the enjoyment of those two shabby pedants in eating[1].

Su Shi (1036-1101)
Zhi Lin (Short Essays)

---

(1) The writer seems to accept the fact that the enjoyment in eating is greater than that in sleeping for many who live at subsistence level.

63. 承天寺夜游

　　元豐六年（1083）十月十二日，夜，解衣欲睡，
月色入戶，欣然起行。念無與樂者，遂至承天寺尋張懷
民，懷民亦未寢，相與步於中庭。庭下如積水空明，水
中藻荇交橫，蓋竹柏影也。何夜無月？何處無竹柏？但
少閑人如吾兩人耳。

　　　　　　　　　　　　　　　　蘇軾《志林》

63. A Night Trip to Heavenly Grace Temple

On the night of the twelfth day of the tenth month, in the sixth year (1083)of the period of Yuan Feng, as I was preparing to go to bed, I noticed the moonlight pouring into my room. I got up in a light mood and finding no one around to share my mood with, I went out to visit Zhang Huaimin at the Temple of Heavenly Grace. Huaimin had also not yet retired, and we both walked in the courtyard. The courtyard had assumed the appearance of a radiant pool of water, with crisscrossing aquatic plants and algae, which were actually formed by the shadows of pines and bamboos. Did the moon not shine every night? Were there no pines and bamboos anywhere else? Not so, just that there were no other leisurely people around like ourselves.

Su Shi (1036-1101)
Zhi Lin (Short Essays)

159

64. 宋璟進諫

　　中宗時（705-710），韋月將告武三思與韋后通。三思諷有司論月將大逆不道。帝詔殺之。宋璟請付獄。帝怒，岸幘出側門，謂璟曰：“朕謂已誅之矣，更何請也？”璟曰：“人言三思亂宮掖，陛下不問，即斬之，臣恐有竊議者，故請按罪方行刑。”帝愈怒。璟曰：“請先誅臣。不然，終不奉詔。”帝乃免月將死，流之嶺南。張嘉貞後為相，閱堂案，見璟危言切議，未嘗不失聲歎息。

　　　　　　　　　　　　　　　　孔平仲《續世說》

160

64. Song Jing's Admonition

During the reign of Emperor Zhongzong (705-710) of the Tang Dynasty, Wei Yuejiang (?-760) accused Wu Sansi of adultery with Empress Wei. Wu abetted some officials to bring a charge of treason and heresy against Wei. The Emperor ordered the death sentence on Wei. Prime Minister Song Jing (663-737) pleaded with the Emperor to put Wei in prison first.

The Emperor became irritated, flew out of the side door without his cap, and said to Song, "I've already ordered to have him killed, why do you speak for him?" Song answered, "Wei reported to you that Wu had intimate relations with the Empress, but you don't look into the matter, and instead you want to have Wei killed immediately. I'm afraid that people would blame you behind your back. Therefore I suggest Your Majesty bring him to trial before executing him."

The Emperor was mad after hearing this. Song said, "If that is the case, please execute me first, since otherwise I shall never carry out the execution order." The Emperor exonerated Wei from death penalty at last and exiled him to Ling Nan (Guangdong) instead.

Later, Zhang Jiazhen became the Prime Minister. Once as he looked through the documents of the court, Song Jing's sharp and reasonable words caught his eyes, he couldn't help sighing with feelings of admiration.

Kong Pingzhong
Xu Shi Shuo (A Sequel to New Accounts of Old Episodes)

65. 逼婚

　　有一新貴少年，有風姿，為貴族之有勢力者所慕，
命十數僕擁致其第。少年欣然而行，略不辭遜。既至，
觀者如堵。須臾，有衣金紫者出曰："某惟一女，亦不
至醜陋，願配君子，可乎？"少年鞠躬謝曰："寒微得
託跡高門，固幸，待更歸家，試與妻商量如何？"眾皆
大笑而散。

彭乘《墨客揮犀》

65. A Forced Marriage

There was a scholar who rose in position recently, and he was also a handsome young man. He caught the attention of an influential nobleman who ordered his servants to bring him to his mansion. The young man did not decline the invitation, and went with them happily. On his arrival, many people crowded round to see him. At that moment, a man dressed in a purple robe and carrying a bag embroidered with a goldfish, came out to greet him, introducing himself with the words: "I have only one daughter, who is not uncomely, and I am looking for a gentleman to marry her to. Would you be interested?"

The young scholar bowed to show his gratitude and replied, "How fortunate it is if one so humble as I should be related to such a high official. Only I must first return to discuss the matter with my wife. I hope you don't mind."

Everybody roared with laughter when they heard his remark.

Peng Cheng
Mo Ke Hui Xi (A Writer's Sketches)

66. 草書

　　張丞相[1]好草聖而不工，流輩皆譏笑之，丞相自若也。一日，得句，索筆絕書，滿紙龍蛇飛動；使其侄錄之，當波險處，侄惘然而止，執所書問曰：「此何字？」丞相熟視久之，亦自不識，詬其侄曰：「胡不早問，致我忘之？」

邢居實《拊掌錄》

---

(1) 張丞相：張齊賢，於宋太宗淳化二年（991）拜吏部侍郎，同中書門下平章事，四年（993）免。真宗即位，再入相，以坐冬至朝會被酒失儀免，為咸平三年（1000）。

66. Cursive Handwriting

Prime Minister Zhang enjoyed writing in the cursive style but his handwriting was too illegible for recognition. All his friends laughed at him for it, but he did not care. One day he thought up a sentence he liked, so he wielded a brush to note it down at once. The paper was filled with lively characters. He asked his nephew to copy it down. While transcribing it, his nephew came to an illegible character and stopped at a loss. He took the paper to his uncle and asked him, "What is this character?" The Prime Minister stared at it for a good while, also failing to figure it out. He scolded his nephew, "Why didn't you ask me earlier before I forgot it?"

Xing Jushi (1068-1087)
Fu Zhang Lu (A Record of Hearty Laughter)

67. 王荊公[1] 簡率

　　王荊公性簡率，不事修飾奉養，衣服垢污，飲食粗惡，一無有擇，自少時則然。蘇明允[2] 著《辨奸》，其言"衣臣虜之衣，食犬彘之食，囚著喪面而談詩書"，以為"不近人情"者，蓋謂是也。然少喜與呂惠穆[3]、韓獻肅兄弟[4] 遊。為館職[5] 時，玉汝[4] 嘗率與同浴於僧寺，潛備新衣一襲，易其敝衣。俟其浴出，俾其從者舉以衣之，而不以告。荊公服之如固有，初不以為異也。及為執政，或言其喜食獐脯者，其夫人聞而疑之，曰："公平日未嘗有擇於飲食，何忽獨嗜此？"因令問左右執事者曰："何以知公之嗜獐脯耶？"曰："每食

---

(1) 王荊公：王安石，封荊國公。
(2) 蘇明允：蘇洵，字明允。
(3) 惠穆：呂公弼諡。
(4) 韓獻肅兄弟：獻肅，韓絳諡；絳弟維、縝皆有名。玉汝為韓縝字。
(5) 館職：唐宋時凡在史館、昭文館、集賢館等處任職·自直館至校勘，都稱館職。

67. Wang Anshi[1] Lived a Simple Life

Wang Anshi (1021-1086) led a simple and unpretentious life. He never cared about how he was dressed or what he ate. He always wore old and worn clothes, and his food was plain and coarse. He took all these things for granted, having lived like that since his youth.

In *The Hypocrites* Su Mingyun described Wang as "being dressed in clothes fit for a slave or captive, eating food fit only for pigs or dogs, and appearing like one in prison or looking as if he were in mourning for the dead, and yet he talks about literature and history." He assumed that Wang was an unnatural oddity due to his outward appearance.

However, when Wang was young, he was close friends with Lu Hui Mu and the Han brothers. As an official in an academy of literature and history he once went with Han Yuru to a temple to bathe. Han had prepared new clothes for him in his ignorance, so that he did not need to wear the old ones any longer. After he emerged from the bath, his servant helped him put on the new suit without saying anything, and Wang wore it without noticing the difference.

Later, Wang was promoted to be vice-prime minister. Somebody at that time stated that Wang liked to eat river deer's meat, but his wife did not believe this and wondered, "He has never been particular about food, how come he suddenly fancies this?" Then she questioned the servants, "How could you be that sure His Excellency likes to eat river deer's meat?" The reply was: "During

---

(1) Wang Anshi: a famous politician, writer and thinker of the Song Dynasty.

不顧他物，而獐脯獨盡，是以知之。"復問："食時置
獐脯何所？"曰："在近匕箸處。"夫人曰："明日姑
易他物近匕箸。"既而果食他物盡，而獐脯固在。而
後，人知其特以其近故食之，而初非有所嗜也。人見其
太甚，或者多疑其偽云。

朱弁《曲洧舊聞》

his meal he only eats the river deer's meat, so it is quite obvious." The lady asked further, "Whereabout is the dish placed on the table?" They said, "Closest to his chopsticks and spoon."

The lady spoke once more, "Tomorrow, place another dish nearest to his chopsticks."

The next day, Wang did not touch the meat of the river deer, but ate only the dish nearest to him. After this everybody realized the truth about the matter, that he merely ate whichever dish was nearest to him but had no particular taste in food. His extreme nonchalance and lack of preference made many people suspect that this was only a front he put on.

Zhu Bian (?-1148)
Qu Wei Jiu Wen (Old Legends of Qu Wei River)

68. 烏巾

荊公退居金陵[1]。蔣山學佛者，俗姓吳，日供灑掃，山下田家子也。一日風墮掛壁舊烏巾，吳舉之，復置於壁。公適見之，謂曰：“乞汝歸遺父。”數日，公問：“幞頭安在？”吳曰：“父，村老，無用，貨於市中，嘗賣得錢三百，供父，感相公之賜也。”公嘆息之，因呼一僕同吳以原價往贖，且戒苟已轉售，即不須訪索。果以弊惡猶存，乃贖以歸。公命取小刀自於巾腳刮磨，粲然黃金也。蓋禁中所賜者，乃復遺吳。

張邦基《墨莊漫錄》

---

(1) 金陵：今江蘇南京。

170

68. The Black Headdress

When Wang Anshi (1021-1086) retired to Jinling (Nanking), a lay Buddhist of Jiang Shan, the son of a peasant family Wu, cleaned the house for him daily. One day a black headdress on the wall was blown off by the wind, Wu picked it up and put it back on the wall. Wang who happened to catch sight of it said, "I'd like to present this headdress to your father."

After a few days, Wang asked, "Is the headdress still in your home?"

Wu replied, "My father is a villager, and he never wears a headdress. So I sold it at the fair for three hundred coppers which I gave to my father. He appreciates your favour very much."

Wang sighed, and sent a servant to the fair with Wu to redeem the headdress for the same price. They were told not to search around far if it had been resold. As they had expected, the headdress had remained there because it looked rather worn-out, so they bought it back. Wang scraped the edge of the headdress with his knife, and the brightness of gold shone through clearly. The gold-rimmed headdress had been an award from the Emperor.

In spite of this, he once more gave the headdress to Wu.

Zhang Bangji
Mo Zhuang Man Lu (Essays of Mo Zhuang)

69. 書換銅器

　　張文潛[1]嘗言：近時印書盛行，而鬻書者往往皆士人，躬自負擔。有一士人盡掊其家所有，約百餘千，買書將以入京[2]。至中途，遇一士人取書目閱之，愛其書，而貧不能得。家有數古銅器，將以貨之。而鬻書者雅有好古器之癖，一見甚喜，乃曰：“毋庸貨也，我將與汝估其值而兩易之。”於是盡以隨行之書，換數十銅器，亟返其家。其妻方訝夫之回疾，視其行李，但見二三布囊，磊硊然鏗鏗有聲。問得其實，乃詈其夫曰：“你換得他這個，幾時近得飯吃！”士人曰：“他換得我那個，也幾時近得飯吃！”因言人之惑也如此，座皆絕倒。

佚名《道山清話》

---

(1) 張文潛：張耒，字文潛。
(2) 京：今河南開封。

69. Books in Exchange for Bronze Vessels

Zhang Wenqian once recounted the following story.

Nowadays publishing books is in fashion and many booksellers are scholars, who often carry heavy loads of books with a shoulder pole. Once there was a scholar who spent all his money to buy books and then carried them to the capital for sale. On the way he met another scholar, who asked if he might see the books. After reading a little, he wished to buy them, but was too poor to afford any. He had some old bronze vessels, which he decided to sell to raise some money for the books. It just so happened that the bookseller was also an antique collector, and as soon as he saw the bronzes, he wished to acquire them. He said at once to the man, "Don't sell these, let us go to get them valued, and you may have the books in exchange for the vessels." In this way, he managed to acquire a large number of bronze objects with the books, and then he hurried back home.

When he arrived home, his wife was surprised to see him return so soon. She checked his baggage to see what he had bought. There was nothing but several large cloth bags, with bulky objects which gave out a clanging sound. When she realized what he had done she was furious, scolding him, "You've got these, now you can eat them instead of rice." The scholar replied, "He got my books and he can eat those as well!" This shows how people can be addicted to their hobbies to the neglect of the livelihood of their families. Many listeners fell off their seats with laughter.

Anonymous
Dao Shan Qing Hua (A Record of Chats at Dao Shan)

70. 黃金釵

僧法一、宗杲，自東都[1] 避亂渡江，各攜一笠。杲笠中有黃金釵，每自檢視。一伺知之，杲起登廁，一亟探釵擲江中。杲還，亡釵，不敢言而色變。一叱之曰：「與汝共學了生死大事，乃眷眷此物耶？我適已為汝投之江流矣。」杲展坐具作禮而行。

陸游《老學庵筆記》

---

(1) 東都：河南開封，亦稱東京。

70. The Gold Hairpin

Two monks, Fayi and Zonggao, were on their way crossing the Yangzi River from Kaifeng so as to dodge the chaos of war. Each of them had a bamboo hat. Zonggao hid a gold hairpin in his hat and checked it every day. Fayi caught sight of this. One day, as Zonggao got up for the latrine, Fayi picked up the hairpin and threw it into the river. When Zonggao returned, he found no hairpin. Though he dared not say a single word, his face turned pale. Fayi scolded him, "You and I have learned to make light of life and death, but how come you are still concerned about such a chip? I have already thrown it into the water on your behalf." Zonggao motioned Fayi to sit down and made an obeisance to him.

Lu You (1125-1210)
Lao Xue An Bi Ji (Notes by the Master of the Lao Xue Study)

71. 此是實數

　　僧行持，明州[1]人，有高行而喜滑稽。嘗住餘姚法性，貧甚，有頌曰："大樹大皮裹，小樹小皮纏；庭前紫荊樹，無皮也過年。"後住雪竇。雪竇在四明，與天童、育王俱號名刹。一日同見新守，守問天童觀老，山中幾僧？對曰："千五百。"又以問育王觀老，對曰："千僧。"末以問持，持拱手曰："百二十。"守曰："三刹名相亞，僧乃如此不同耶？"持復拱手曰："敝院是實數。"守為撫掌。

　　　　　　　　　　　　　陸游《老學庵筆記》

---

(1) 明州：浙江寧波。

71. The Actual Number

A monk called Xingchi, from Mingzhou, had great accomplishments and a good sense of humour.

He was very poor when he lived at the Faxing Temple, but he comforted himself, saying, "Big trees have thick skin; small trees have thin skin. But the wisteria in the garden has been living on year after year without skin."

Later he was settled at the Xuedou Monastery. In Siming, Xuedou was as renowned as the Tiantong and Yuwang monasteries. One day Xingchi and the elders of Tiantong and Yuwang were interviewed by the new governor, who asked the elder of Tiantong, "How many monks do you have?"

"One thousand five hundred," the elder replied.

Then the governor asked the elder of Yuwang the same question.

"One thousand," he answered.

At last it was the turn of Xingchi, who saluted and said, "One hundred and twenty." The governor said, "Your monasteries are of the same high prestige, but why do the numbers of monks differ so much?" Xingchi saluted again and remarked, "What I gave is the actual number!" The governor applauded amusedly.

Lu You (1125-1210)
Lao Xue An Bi Ji (Notes by the Master of the Lao Xue Study)

72. 不了事漢

　　秦會之[1]當國，有殿前司軍人施全者，伺其入朝，持斬馬刀邀於望仙橋下斫之。斷轎子一柱，而不能傷，誅死。其後秦每出，輒以親兵五十人持梃衛之。初，斬全於市，觀者甚眾，有一人朗言曰：「此不了事漢，不斬何為！」聞者皆笑。

陸游《老學庵筆記》

---

(1) 秦會之：秦檜，字會之。

72. The Brainless Idiot

Qin Gui (1090-1155)[1] was in power. One day, when he was on his way to court, a general called Shi Quan was waiting for him under the Wangxian Bridge with a sabre in hand. When Qin approached, Shi stabbed at him, but only cut off a post of the sedan. So Shi was put to death. Since then, whenever Qin was out, he would have 50 soldiers keep guard, holding sticks around him.

When Shi Quan was about to be beheaded before the public, there was a tremendous crowd of spectators. One among them went off loudly, "This brainless idiot, why not behead him!" All those who heard this laughed it off.

Lu You (1125-1210)
Lao Xue An Bi Ji (Notes by the Master of Lao Xue Study)

---

(1) Qin Gui: Prime Minister of the Southern Song Dynasty (1127-1279). He advocated peace negotiation with Jin, an invading tribe, and was therefore much hated by the people.

73. 白席

　　北方民家吉凶，輒有相禮者，謂之“白席”，多鄙俚可笑。韓魏公[1]自樞密歸鄴。赴一姻家禮席，偶取盤中一荔枝欲啗之，白席者遽唱曰：“資政喫荔枝，請眾客同喫荔枝。”魏公憎其喋喋，因置之不復取。白席者又曰：“資政惡發也。請眾客放下荔枝。”魏公為一笑。

陸游《老學庵筆記》

---

(1) 韓魏公：宋韓琦封魏國公。

73. The Master of Ceremonies

In the north people who conducted ceremonies on occasions of jubilation or condolences were known as the *baixi*. They must act snobbishly, and play the fool. Once, Han Chi, the Duke of Wei, returned to his home-town of Ye, where he was invited to a celebration by a relative. At the party he picked up a lychee to eat, and immediately the *baixi* roared out: "His Excellency has picked up a lychee, everybody please do the same." Han was disgusted at this flippancy and replaced the lychee without tasting it. At this the *baixi* burst out again: "His Excellency is not amused. Would all the guests also please replace their lychees?" At this Han just laughed it away.

Lu You (1125-1210)
Lao Xue An Bi Ji (Notes by the Master of Lao Xue Study)

74. 霍將軍

吳興士子六人入京師赴省試，共買紗一百匹，一僕負之。晚行汴堤上，逢黥卒，蓬首鼇面，貿貿然出於榛中。見眾至，有喜色，左顧而嘯。俄數人相繼出，挾槊持刀，氣貌兇悍。皆知其賊也，雖懼而不可脫。同行霍秀才者，長大勇健，能角抵技擊，鄉里目為霍將軍。與諸人約勿走，使列立於後，獨操所策短棒奮而前。羣賊輕笑，視如几上肉。霍連奮擊，輒中其膝，皆迎杖仆地不能興，然後得去。前行十餘里，過巡檢營，入告之。巡檢大喜曰：“此輩出沒近地，殺人至多。官立賞名，捕不可獲，何意一旦成擒？”邀諸客小駐，自率眾馳而東。儼然在地，宛轉反側，凡七八輩。盡執縛以歸，護送府而厚謝客。五士謂霍：“非與君偕來，已落賊手

74. General Huo

Six scholars of Wu Xing headed for the capital to take the imperial examination. They had bought a hundred feet of linen and had a servant carry it. One night while walking along the embankment of the Yellow River, they ran into a tattooed rogue with a rough appearance, who was crouching in a bush. This rogue began to whistle excitedly when he saw them coming. Several men appeared from the bushes around, all carrying weapons and looking fierce. To their horror, the scholars recognized them as bandits, but could find nowhere to escape. One of them, named Huo, was a strong wrestler, and had earned the nickname of General Huo. He asked his companions not to escape but to stand behind him, while he alone stepped forward towards the bandits with a cudgel to defend himself. The bandits sneered, considering him an easy opponent, but Huo fought back furiously, striking at their knees. All the bandits were beaten to the ground, unable to get up, and thus the scholars managed to get away.

After continuing for a dozen miles, they reached a police station and made a report. The inspector was most relieved, saying, "These rogues have been haunting this area for some time and have killed many people. The authorities have put a price on their heads, but no one has been successful in catching them. Can we really seize them all at the same time?"

He asked them to remain there for a while, and he led a band of armed men eastwards. As expected, more than half a dozen of the bandits were still there writhing on the ground in pain. The inspector had them bound up and escorted them back. He offered the guests a handsome reward. The other five scholars said to Huo, "If we hadn't travelled with you, we would have fallen into the hands

矣。"霍曰："吾若獨行，亦必不免。諸君雖不施力，
然立衛吾後，無反顧憂，此所以能勝也。"

洪邁《夷堅志》

of the bandits." Huo replied, "Had I been alone, it would have happened to me as well. With you all standing firmly behind me, even though you didn't help me fight the bandits, I lost all my fear, and that was how I could defeat them."

Hong Mai (1123-1202)
Yi Jian Zhi (The Yi Jian Records)

75. 奮不顧身而得生

　　建炎庚戌（1130）胡騎犯江西，郡縣村落之民望而畏之，多束手斃。間有奮不顧身者，則往往得志焉，雖婦女亦勇為之。其過豐城劍池也，鐵騎行正道，通宵不絕，蓋使我眾聞其聲，而不測多寡耳。一騎挾兩女子獨穿林間，女指謂避者言可擊，於是眾舉梃椿之而墜，旋碎其腦，馬嘶鳴不已，似尋其主，眾逐而委之井，遂脫。又，胡擄一婦使汲井，婦素富家子，辭不能。胡呦呦怒罵，奪瓶器低頭取水，婦推其背，失足於井中。餘干民艾公子全家遭劫虜，兩胡燃火，將焚厥居。艾嘿念若蕩為丘墟，萬一獲脫，將無所歸。乃呼其子，齊奮

75. Fight Back to Survive

In the year Geng Xu of the Jian Yan period (1130), the cavalry of Jin[1] invaded Jiang Xi. The inhabitants of the region were extremely afraid, and waited to meet their fate. Among them were some who had the courage to fight back, and on occasions they defeated the enemy. Even women were involved in the battles, showing no less bravery. Once as a small number of cavalrymen rode past Jian Chi of Feng City, they made a great clamour all night long in order to bluff the local people, so that they could not guess their numbers.

A rider caught two girls and dragged them away on horseback into the forest. The girls pointed out to fleeing people that the horseman was vulnerable. So the crowd clubbed him off the horse and broke his skull. His horse whined incessantly as if it was seeking for its old master, so the people threw it into a well to avoid discovery and escaped away.

Another time the Jin soldiers caught a woman, whom they forced to draw water from a well. As she was from a rich family, she replied that she had no idea of how to draw water. A soldier scolded her angrily and, seizing the bucket, leant over the well to draw water himself. She pushed him straight down the well.

In Yu Gan the family of Ai were captured by the enemy. Two of the soldiers lit torches and were about to burn down the dwellings. When Ai saw this, he feared that they would be made homeless in case they were freed. So he ordered his sons to resist, until

---

(1) Jin: a tribe invading China from the north in the 12th century and put an end to the Northern Song Dynasty (960-1127).

梃縱擊垂困，取胡腰刀截其首，一家遂全。

洪邁《夷堅志》

they managed to overpower the soldiers and cut off their heads with their sabres. Thus the family managed to save themselves.

Hong Mai (1123-1202)
Yi Jian Zhi (The Yi Jian Records)

76. 鬭牛圖

　　馬正惠公[1]嘗珍其所藏戴嵩[2]"鬭牛圖"，暇日展曝於廳前。有輸租氓見而竊笑，公疑之，問其故。對曰："農非知畫，乃識真牛。方其鬭時，夾尾於髀間，雖壯夫膂力不能出之，此圖皆舉其尾，似不類矣。"公為之歎服。

曾敏行《獨醒雜志》

---

(1) 馬正惠公：馬知節，諡正惠。
(2) 戴嵩：八世紀下半期（唐代後期）畫家，與韓滉（723-787）同
　　時，以畫牛著名。

76. A Painting of Fighting Bulls

Ma Zhijie (955-1019) highly treasured a painting of fighting bulls by the painter Dai Song, which he possessed. Once while he was relaxing, he aired the painting in the sunshine at the front of the hall. One of his tenant farmers, who came to pay rent, saw it and laughed up his sleeve. Ma suspected the man of some mischief, and asked him why he had been laughing. The man replied, "I'm a farmer and I know nothing about paintings, but I do know about bulls. When they fight, they always press their tails between their legs. Even a strong man cannot pull the tail out straight. But in this picture the bulls stick out their tails, so it is not life-like."

Ma could not but believe his words.

Zeng Minxing (?-1175)
Du Xing Za Zhi (Notes Written While Awake Alone)

77. 文山書為北人所重

　　平江[1]趙昇卿之姪總管號中山者云：近有親朋過河間府，因憩道傍，燒餅主人延入其家。內有小低閣，壁帖四詩，乃文宋瑞[2]筆也。漫云：「此字寫得也好，以兩貫鈔換兩幅與我，如何？」主人笑曰：「此吾傳家寶也，雖一錠鈔一幅亦不可博。咱們祖上亦是宋民，流落在此。趙家三百年天下，只有這一個官人，豈可輕易把與人邪？文丞相前年過此與我寫的，真是寶物也。」斯人樸直可敬如此。所謂公論在野人也。

周密《癸辛雜識》

---

(1) 平江：宋設平江軍，治所在今蘇州。
(2) 文宋瑞：文天祥，字宋瑞，號文山，官至右丞相，抗元被俘，送京師（今北京），不屈，為元世祖忽必烈所殺。

77. The Priceless Calligraphy

Zhongshan, a nephew of Zhao Shengqing of Pingjiang, and a military commander, once told the following story.

A relative of mine was on his way to Hejian County, and while he was resting by the roadside, a baker invited him to his house. He arrived to find a garret with a low ceiling and on whose walls were hung four poems, the calligraphy being that of Wen Tianxiang (1236-1282)[1]. He made a casual remark: "Both the poetry and the calligraphy are excellent! Would you sell me two for two *guan*[2]?"

The host smiled, "This is my inheritance, and I would never part with it, even if you offered me much more money." He added, "My ancestry goes back to the Song Dynasty. We had become so poor that we had to move here. During the three hundred years of reign of the Zhao rulers[3], there has been only one true statesman, and this is his calligraphy. How could I allow this to pass into the hands of another person? Prime Minister Wen wrote these for me the year before last, when he passed by here, so they are a priceless treasure to me!"

The man was simple and honest, worthy of high respect. That is why people say: public opinion is certainly the best judge.

Zhou Mi (1232-1298)
Gui Xin Za Shi (Records in the Years from Gui to Xin)

---

(1) Wen Tianxiang: the last Prime Minister of the Song Dynasty (960-1279) who was famous for his patriotism. He was also renowned for his poetry and calligraphy.
(2) 1 *guan*= 1,000 coppers
(3) Zhao rulers: the family name of the emperors of the Song Dynasty was Zhao.

78. 縣令明察

　　縣有民將出商，既登舟，伺一奴久不至。舟人見其
單子也，地復僻寂，忽發惡念，急起擠之水，攜其貲
歸，更詣商家擊門，問商何不行。商妻遣視舟，無有
也。問奴，奴言至舟不見主人，莫知所之也。乃始以聞
之縣，遠[1]舟人鄰比，訽詢反復，卒無狀。由是歷年莫
決。至此令因屏人獨詢商妻，始舟人來問時言語情狀乃
若何。妻云：“夫去久，舟人來擊門，門未啟，遽呼
曰：‘娘子，如何官人久不來下船？’言只此耳。”令
卻屏婦，召舟人詢狀，其語同。令笑曰：“是矣，殺人
者汝，汝已自服，無須他證。”舟人譁曰：“何服
邪？”令曰：“明知官人不在家，所以叩門稱娘子。豈

---

(1) 遠：據《叢書集成》影印《歷代小史》本，費解，似為“逮”
　　字之訛。

194

78. The Prefect of Keen Perception

A man on a business trip was waiting on board a boat for a servant who did not turn up for a long time. Noticing that he was alone and the place was rather out of reach, the boatman harboured an evil idea. He pushed the businessman into the water and robbed him of all his possessions. Afterwards, he even went to the house of the businessman, knocked on the door and asked why the man had not set off.

The wife of the businessman sent her servant to look for her husband in the boat, but failed to find him. When asked, the servant said he had not seen his master as he reached the boat.

The case was reported to the prefect, who brought the boatman and his neighbours to trial, but to no avail.

So the case remained unsettled for years until one day the prefect questioned the wife alone about the situation when the boatman came to her house. The wife replied, "After my husband had left for a good while, the boatman came and knocked at the door. Before I had opened the door, he shouted, 'Lady, why hasn't your husband come on board the boat yet?' That's all that he said."

Ordering the woman aside, the prefect questioned the boatman, whose confession was identical to the woman's. The prefect laughed, "Yes, the murderer must be you. You have already admitted it, we don't need any other evidence." The boatman was astonished and shouted, "How come?" The prefect answered, "You were aware that the man couldn't be at home, therefore you immediately called to the lady of the house while knocking at the

有見人不來而即知其不在乃不呼之者乎？"舟人駭伏，
遂正其法。

祝允明《野記》

door. How could you have known that the man was not in and called to his wife instead, just because you hadn't seen him in your boat?"

The boatman pleaded guilty in awe, and it wasn't long before his execution.

Zhu Yunming (1460-1526)
Ye Ji (Legends)

79. 相疑為鬼

　　吾杭八字橋，相傳多邪穢蠱於行客。東有浴肆，夜半即有湯。一人獨行遇雨。驀有避雨傘下者。其人意此必鬼也，至橋上，排之於水，乃急走。見浴肆有燈，入避之。頃一人淋漓而至，且喘曰：「帶傘鬼擠我於河中，幾為溺死矣。」兩人相語，則皆誤矣。

　　又一人宵行無燈而微雨。聞後有屐聲，回頭見一大頭，身長二尺許。佇立觀之，頭亦隨立。及行，頭亦行。及趨，頭亦趨。其人大恐，亟馳至浴肆，排闥直入；未及掩門，頭亦隨入。此人幾落膽矣。引燭觀之，乃一小兒也。蓋以大斗障雨，亦懼鬼，故緊隨之耳。是

198

79. Suspecting Each Other of Being Ghosts

There was a bridge called Baizi in Hangzhou, my hometown, and a popular belief was that it was haunted by unfriendly ghosts. On the eastern side was a public bathhouse which provided hot water in the evenings.

One day a man happened to be caught in the rain as he travelled alone. Suddenly somebody took shelter under his umbrella, and he mistook him for a ghost. When they reached the bridge he shoved the stranger into the river. He hurried on until he saw the lights on in the bathhouse and rushed inside. Not long afterwards another man arrived, soaked to the skin. He said breathlessly, "A ghost with an umbrella pushed me into the river and I was nearly drowned." Speaking to each other, both men realized that they had mistaken each other for a ghost.

Another man, travelling without a lamp at night in the rain, heard footsteps behind him. Turning around, he saw behind him a large head with a body of only two feet tall. He stopped to look at it, and the head also stopped. When he started walking, the head did likewise. He then hastened forward, but the head also hurried after him. He was so afraid that he ran as fast as he could, until he reached the bathhouse. He dashed inside, and before he could close the door the head rushed in after him. He was scared out of his wits. When he lit a candle to see what it was, he found a child with its head covered with a large basket to keep out the rain. As the child was afraid of ghosts he had followed the man closely all

亦為錯者也。向使此四人各散去不白，則以為真鬼矣。
今之見鬼者，何卒懼也哉？

郎瑛《七修類稿》

the way. This was yet another false alarm.

If these people had never discovered the truth, they would really have believed that there were ghosts. Why should people who think that they see ghosts be afraid?

Lang Ying (1487-?)
Qi Xiu Lei Gao (A Notebook in Seven Parts)

80. 告荒

有告荒者，官問："麥收若干？"曰："三分。"
又問："棉花若干？"曰："二分。"又問："稻收若
干？"曰："二分。"官怒曰："有七分年歲，尚捏稱
荒耶？"對曰："某活一百幾十歲矣，實未見如此奇
荒。"官問之。曰："某年七十餘，長子四十餘，次子
三十餘，合而算之，有一百幾十歲。"哄堂大笑。

楊慎《丹鉛雜錄》

80. Reporting Famine

A man reported a famine to an official. The official asked, "How much wheat have you harvested?"

"Thirty percent of the normal yield," the man replied.

"How much cotton?"

"Twenty percent."

"How much rice?"

"Twenty percent."

The official got mad, "You've already had seventy percent of the harvest, how dare you trump up famine then?"

The man said, "I've never seen such an extraordinary famine in my life of a hundred and several scores of years."

"How could you have lived so long?" asked the official.

"Look, I'm over seventy years old. My eldest son is over forty and my second son is over thirty. The total is a hundred and several scores of years." All the people hearing this burst out laughing.

Yang Shen (1488-1559)
Dan Qian Za Lu (Notes)

81. 點選秀女

　　隆慶二年（1568）戊辰正月元旦大風，走石飛沙，天地昏黑。湖市新碼頭官船起火，沿燒民居二千餘家，官民船舫焚者三四百隻，死者四十餘人。至初八、九日，民間訛言朝廷點選秀女。自湖州而來，人家女子七八歲以上、二十歲以下無不婚嫁。不及擇配，東送西迎，街市接踵，勢如抄奪。甚則畏官府禁之，黑夜潛行，惟恐失曉；歌笑哭泣之聲，喧嚷達旦。千里鼎沸。無問大小長幼美惡貧富，以出門得偶即為大幸。雖山谷村落之僻，士夫詩禮之家，亦皆不免。時偶一大將官抵北關，放炮三聲，民間愈驚慌，走曰：“朝廷使太監至矣！”倉皇激變，幾至於亂。至十三日，上司出榜嚴

81. A Rumour about Choosing the Royal Maids

On New Year's Day of the second year of Long Qing (1568) a gale erupted, sending stones and sand flying in the air and darkening the whole sky.

The royal fleet at the new dock of Hushi caught fire and the blaze engulfed more than two thousand dwellings. Over three hundred ships and boats, both official and private, were destroyed, and more than forty people had died in the conflagration.

On the eighth and ninth days of the month a rumour spread among the folks that the court would send eunuchs to pick young maids, and the exercise would start in Huzhou.

Many girls between the age of seven and twenty were hastily found husbands, and if a match could not be found, they would be busily sent or hidden away. It seemed that everybody was in a rush for marriage as if a confiscation was going on. Some people who were afraid that their actions would be banned by the government often acted in the middle of the night. Thus the sounds of happy weddings and weeping in despair raged through the night.

The whole district was boiling with excitement fuelled by the events taking place. It was of no consequence as to the age, look, background, or suitability of the husband, both the rich and the poor deemed it lucky to find a spouse for their girls. Those living in remote villages and households of nobility had to submit to the same fate.

One day, a general arrived at the northern gate of the city and the cannons were fired three times as a salute. People hearing the reports panicked and rushed about announcing to everybody that the court eunuchs had arrived. The commotion nearly turned into a riot.

禁，猶不能止，真人間之大變也。未幾而知其偽，悔恨嗟歎之聲則又盈於室家，然亦無及矣。愚民無知搖惑，此甚可笑也。此風直播於江西、閩、廣，極於邊海而止，又何其遠也！一富家偶雇一錫工在家造鑞器。至半夜，有女不得其配，又不敢出門擇人，乃呼錫工曰：「急起，急起！可成親也。」錫工睡夢中茫然無知，及起而摩搓兩眼，則堂前燈燭輝煌，主翁之女已艷妝待聘矣。大出不意。

田藝蘅《留青日札》

On the thirteenth day of the month the local government put up notices forbidding the spreading of further rumours, but failed to bring it to an end. The hectic situation was indeed a catastrophe for the people. Before long when it was evidenced to be mere rumour, the moans of regret arose. However in any case it was too late to regret. It was really ridiculous that the naive folks were fooled out of ignorance. Yet this rumour spread from Jiang Xi, Min and Guang to sea coasts far away. How incredible it was!

One story was recounted as follows: A rich family had hired a tinsmith to make tin wares for their household. As they had failed to find any man suitable for their daughter and were afraid to go out to find one in case they were discovered, they called the tinsmith in the middle of the night: "Get up! Get up! It's time for your wedding!" The tinsmith, aware of nothing, was woken up from sleep. While he was rubbing his sleepy eyes, the whole house was brightly lit with candles, and the daughter of the household was beautifully adorned, waiting for him to become her husband. That was simply far beyond his expectation.

Tian Yiheng
Liu Qing Ri Zha (The Liu Qing Diary)

82. 箭喻

　　吐谷渾[1]阿豺有疾，召母弟慕利延曰：「汝取一枝箭折之乎。」慕利延折之。「汝取十九枝箭折之。」慕利延不能折。阿豺曰：「汝曹知乎：單者易折。眾者難摧。戮力一心，然後社稷可固。」阿豺有子二十人，終生同心協力。

　　　　　　　　　　　　　　　李贄《初潭集》

---

(1) 吐谷渾：隋唐之際建國於今青海北部和新疆東南部的少數民族，龍朔三年（661）為吐蕃所滅。

82. The Metaphor of Arrows

The chief of the tribe Tuyuhun, Acai, was badly ill. He said to his uncle Muliyan, "Please get an arrow, and break it. " Muliyan did accordingly.

"Get nineteen arrows, and break them together."

Muliyan failed to do so.

The chief remarked to his family, "You should know that a single piece is easy to break, but a mass is hard to destroy. When all of you are united, our tribe will be impregnable."

Acai had twenty sons. They worked together with one heart throughout their lives.

Li Zhi (1527-1602)
Chu Tan Ji (The Chu Tan Collection of Anecdotes)

83. 悦諛

　　粵令性悅諛，每布一政，羣下交口贊譽，令乃歡，一吏欲阿其意，故從旁與人偶語曰：「凡居民上者，類喜人諛，惟吾主不然，視人譽蔑如耳。」其令耳之，亟召隸前，撫膺高蹈，嘉賞不已，曰：「嘻，知余心者惟汝。」自是昵之有加。

劉元卿《應諧錄》

83. Intoxicated with Blarney

The prefect of Yue liked others to be subservient before him. Whatever policy he announced, his subordinates would pour compliments upon him, which delighted him greatly. A servant of his, who wished to curry favour with him, whispered to his associates, "All those holding high positions enjoy flattery, except our master, who views such behaviour with contempt." These words caught the ears of the prefect, who called the servant before him. Patting him on the back and lavishing praises on him, he said, "My dear boy, only you understand me fully." Since then the prefect favoured that servant in particular.

Liu Yuanqing (1544-1609)
Ying Xie Lu (A Record of Banters)

84. 鍾馗吃鬼

　　鍾馗專好吃鬼，其妹與他做生日，寫禮帖云："酒一樽，鬼兩個，送與哥哥做點剁；哥哥若嫌禮物少，連挑擔的是三個。"鍾馗命人將三個鬼俱送庖人烹之。擔上鬼看挑擔者曰："我們死是本等，你如何挑這個擔子？"

　　　　　　　　　　　　　　　趙南星《笑贊》

84. Zhong Kui Eats Ghosts

Zhong Kui specially enjoyed eating ghosts. His sister made a present to him on his birthday, in the giftlist standing: "A jar of liquor and two ghosts, for you, brother, as snacks. If that is not enough, the carrier is the third."

Zhong Kui had the three ghosts brought to the kitchen. The two ghosts said to the carrier ghost: "Our death has been doomed, but what did you carry this load for?[1]"

Zhao Nanxing (1550-1627)
Xiao Zan (Ode to Laughter)

---

(1) This implies that the third ghost need not have been submitted to the same fate of being cooked had it not carried the other two to Zhong Kui.

85. 打差別

　　郡人趙世傑半夜睡醒，語其妻曰：“我夢中與他家婦女交接，不知婦女亦有此夢否？”其妻曰：“男子婦人，有甚差別？”世傑遂將其妻打了一頓。至今留下俗語云：“趙世傑，半夜起來打差別。”

趙南星《笑贊》

85. Beat Out the Difference

A man called Zhao Shijie woke up one night and told his wife, "I dreamed a dream that I was in bed with another woman. Do women have similar dreams?" The wife said, "I don't see why there should be difference between man and woman." Zhao beat her up as a result.

Since then folks say, "Zhao Shijie got up at night, and beat out the difference."

Zhao Nanxing (1550-1627)
Xiao Zan (Ode to Laughter)

86. 尊奉三教

一人尊奉三教，塑像先孔子，次老君，次釋迦。道士見之，即移老君於中。僧來又移釋迦於中。士來仍移孔子於中。三聖自相謂曰：“我們自好好的，卻被人搬來搬去，搬得我們壞了。”

趙南星《笑贊》

86. Reverence for Three Religions

A man showed reverence for three religions—Confucianism, Taoism and Buddhism. He put the statue of Confucius in the middle, the statue of Laozi on the left, and the statue of Buddha on the right. A Taoist priest came over and shifted the statue of Laozi to the middle. Then a Buddhist monk came over and placed the statue of Buddha in the middle. Later a Confucianist came over and shifted the statue of Confucius to the middle again. The three saints sighed out to one another: "We got on pretty well together before, but now they've moved us around and upset us!"

Zhao Nanxing (1550-1627)
Xiao Zan (Ode to Laughter)

87. 做屁文章的秀才

　　一秀才數盡，去見閻王，閻王偶放一屁，秀才即獻屁頌一篇曰："高竦金臀，弘宣寶氣，依稀乎絲竹之音，仿佛乎麝蘭之味，臣立下風，不勝馨香之至。"閻王大喜，增壽十年，即時放回陽間。十年限滿，再見閻王。這秀才志氣舒展，望森羅殿搖擺而上，閻王問是何人，小鬼說道："是那做屁文章的秀才。"

趙南星《笑贊》

87. A *Xiucai*[(1)] Who Wrote the Farting Article

A *xiucai* died, and was interviewed by the King of Hell. Suddenly the King broke wind, and the *xiucai* immediately wrote an ode to the fart: "Stick up Your Majesty's golden hip, and send out the precious wind. It sounds like mild music, and smells of musk and orchid. I stood facing windward, with its aroma intoxicated."

The ode put the King in royal spirits. He quickly let the *xiucai* have another ten years in the world.

Ten years later, the *xiucai* came to see the King of Hell again. At this time the *xiucai* strutted into the Palace of Hell smugly. The King wondered who he was, and a ghost said, "He is the rhymester who wrote the farting article."

Zhao Nanxing (1550-1627)
Xiao Zan (Ode to Laughter)

---

(1). *Xiucai*: one who passed the imperial examination at the county level in the Ming and Qing dynasties.

88. 不誤反誤

　　有一狼子，生平多逆父旨，父臨死囑曰：“必葬我
水中。”冀其逆命，得葬土中。至是狼子曰：“生平逆
父命，今死不敢違旨也。”乃築沙潭水心以葬。

　　　　　　　　　　　馮夢龍《古今譚概》

88. Obey and Disobey

One disobedient son often went against his father's wishes. At last, on his deathbed, the father told his son, "Bury me in water." Expecting his son to disobey again, he had requested the opposite of what he really wished for, as he hoped to be buried in the ground.

But the son thought to himself: "I have always disobeyed my father, but this time how can I disobey him again at his death?" So, after his father died, he buried him in the sands of the river.

Feng Menglong (1574-1646)
Gu Jin Tan Gai (Chatting about the Present and the Past)

89. 劉禪⁽¹⁾

司馬文王⁽²⁾問劉禪：“思蜀否？”禪曰：“此間樂，不思。”郤正教禪：“若再問，宜泣對曰：‘先墓在蜀，無日不思。’”會王復問，禪如正言，因閉眼。王曰：“何乃似郤正語？”禪驚視曰：“誠如尊命。”

馮夢龍《古今譚概》

---

(1) 劉禪：蜀後主。魏滅蜀，遷洛陽。
(2) 司馬文王：司馬昭，魏封文王。

89. Liu Chan

Premier Sima Zhao once asked Liu Chan, "Do you miss Shu[1]?" Liu Chan replied, "No, I'm happy here."

Que Zheng later advised Liu Chan, "If asked again, you'd better weep a little, and say to him that the tombs of your ancestors arc all in Shu and that you think about them every day."

On another occasion, when the premier asked him the same question, Liu Chan replied in the way Que Zheng had suggested, and shut his eyes to feign weeping.

The premier responded saying, "How odd! But you seem to be speaking the exact words of Zheng."

Liu Chan opened his eyes in surprise and, staring straight ahead, said, "Your Excellency is right."

Feng Menglong(1574-1646)
Gu Jin Tan Gai (Chatting about the Present and the Past)

---

(1) Shu: the Kingdom of Shu Han (221-263), one of the Three Kingdoms at that time. Liu Chan was the second and last king of Shu. After Shu was conquered, he was removed from Chengdu, the capital of Shu, to Luoyang.

90. 薑生樹上

　　楚人有生而不識薑者，曰：“此從樹上結成。”或曰：“從土裏生成。”其人固執己見，曰：“請與子以十人為質，以所乘驢為賭。”已而遍問十人，皆曰：“土裏出也。”其人啞然失色曰：“驢則付汝，薑還樹生。”

江盈科《雪濤小説》

224

90. Ginger Still Grows on Trees

A man of the State of Chu didn't know about ginger, and once he said, "It grows on trees." But someone put him right, saying, "No, it doesn't, it grows in the earth."

This man persisted in his belief and declared, "Let's ask ten persons, I bet you this donkey I'm riding on that I'm right." So they asked around, and everyone replied, "It grows in the earth."

The man's face paled when he heard this. However he said, "You may have my donkey, but ginger still grows on trees."

Jiang Yingke
Xue Tao Xiao Shuo (Stories of Xue Tao)

91. 湖心亭看雪

　　崇禎五年（1632）十二月，余往西湖。大雪三日，湖中人鳥聲俱絕。是日更定矣，余拏一小舟，擁毳衣爐火，獨往湖心亭看雪。霧淞沆碭，天與雲、與山、與水，上下一白，湖上影子，惟長堤一痕、湖心亭一點、余與舟一芥，舟中人兩三粒而已。到亭上，有兩人鋪氈對坐，一童子燒酒爐正沸。見余大喜曰："湖中焉得更有此人！"拉余同飲。余強飲三大白而別。問其姓氏，是金陵人，客此。及下船，舟子喃喃曰："莫說相公癡，更有癡似相公者。"

張岱，《陶庵夢憶》

91. Enjoying the Snow Scenery

In December of the fifth year of Chong Zhen, I visited the West Lake. It had been snowing heavily for three days on end. The lake was in absolute quietude. Not even a voice of a bird singing could be heard.

In the evening I took a boat, and wrapped in a fur coat, I sat beside the stove in the boat. Thus I went alone to the pavilion in the centre of the lake to look at the snow. A mist spread and enveloped everything. The sky, the clouds, the hills and the lake blended in a stretch of white. The only shadows on the lake were the dam like a trace on the surface of the lake, the pavilion like a dot, myself and the boat like a leaf of grass and the people in the boat like a few seeds. As we reached the pavilion, two people already sat there upon a blanket. A servant was warming the wine, and the pot began to boil. Seeing me, they were very pleased, saying, "Who would ever think that there would be others like us coming out to the lake?" They invited me to drink, and I downed three large cups before parting. I asked them their names and they only said they were travellers from Jinling. As I reboarded the boat, I overheard the boatman murmur, "One might say that you are a queer sort, but there are others just as queer."

Zhang Dai (1597-1679)
Tao An MengYi (Memory of Dreams in Tao Recluse)

92. 大鐵椎傳

　　大鐵椎，不知何許人，北平⁽¹⁾陳子燦省兄河南，與
遇宋將軍家。宋懷慶青華鎮人，工技擊，七省好事者皆
來學，人以其雄健呼宋將軍云。宋弟子高信之，亦懷慶
人，多力善射，長子燦七歲，少同學，故嘗與過宋將
軍。時座上有健啖客，貌甚寢，右脅夾大鐵椎，重四五
十斤，飲食拱揖不暫去，柄鐵摺疊環複如鎖上練，引之
長丈許，與人罕言語，語類楚聲，扣其鄉及姓字，皆不
答。既同寢，夜半，客曰："吾去矣！"言訖不見。子

---

(1) 北平：今北京。

92. Big Iron-Hammer

Once upon a time there was a stranger nicknamed Big Iron-hammer. No one had the least idea where he came from. Once Chen Zican, on his way from Beijing to call on his brother in Henan, ran into Big Iron-hammer at a General Song's home. General Song, so-called, was a native of Qinghua town in Huaiqing. He was skilled at boxing. Boxing enthusiasts came from seven provinces nearby to practise under him. Being considered very strong and powerful, he was known as "General Song". One of Song's pupils, Gao Xinzhi, from Huaiqing as well, was strong and adept in archery. He was seven years older than Chen Zican, and they were school friends when young. As a result, Chen got a chance to meet General Song through Gao.

At that time, there was a stranger at General Song's, who had an amazing appetite and whose appearance was terrifying. He held a big iron hammer weighing 40 to 50 catties under his right arm and never put it down, not even when he drank, ate or saluted. On the handle of the hammer was a string of interlocking rings, like a heavy chain. When fully extended, the hammer, plus this chain, was longer than a *zhang*[1]. This guy seldom talked with others, but when he spoke, the accent of the Chu dialect could be discerned. When he was asked about his hometown and his name, he just gave no answer.

While sleeping with other roommates at midnight one day, the stranger said, "I'm going." Scarcely had he uttered the words

---

(1) 1 *zhang*=3 meters approximately

燦見窗戶皆閉，驚問信之，信之曰："客初至，不冠
不韈，以藍手巾裹頭，足纏白布，大鐵椎外，一物無
所持，而腰多白金，吾與將軍俱不敢問也。"子燦寐而
醒，客則鼾睡炕上矣。一日，辭宋將軍曰："吾始聞汝
名，以為豪，然皆不足用，吾去矣。"將軍強留之。乃
曰："吾嘗奪取諸響馬物，不順者輒擊殺之，眾魁請長
其羣，吾又不許，是以讎我，久居此，禍必及汝，今夜
半，方期我決鬥某所。"宋將軍欣然曰："吾騎馬挾矢
以助戰"。客曰："止，賊能且眾，吾欲護汝，則不快
吾意。"宋將軍故自負，且欲觀客所為，力請客。客不
得已，與偕行。將至鬥處，送將軍登空堡上，曰："但
觀之，慎勿聲，令賊知汝也。"時雞鳴月落，星光照曠
野，百步見人。客馳下，吹觱篥數聲。頃之，賊二十餘
騎四面集，步行負弓矢從者百許人。一賊提刀縱馬奔客

230

when he disappeared. Presently Chen noticed that the windows and the door remained closed. He asked Gao about it with astonishment. Gao said, "At the beginning when the guy arrived, he wore no hat and no socks. He covered his head with a blue handkerchief and his feet with a piece of white cloth. He took almost nothing with him but a big iron hammer, Nevertheless he carried a lot of silver ingots in his pocket. General Song and I dared not ask any questions of him." Chen fell asleep again. When he woke up, the stranger was snoring in bed.

One day Big Iron-hammer bid farewell to General Song, saying, "When I first heard of your name, I thought highly of you, but now I find you are simply a rush candle, so I'm leaving." General Song urged him to stay, then the guy went on to say, "I grab bandits' fortune. When they thwart me, I just kill them. They invited me to be their boss, but I refused them, therefore they hate me. If I settle down here too long, they might harass you. The robbers expect me to duel with them somewhere tonight." General Song said in delight, "Well, I feel like riding there carrying my bow to support you." The stranger remarked, "No, thanks. The robbers are smart and have a large gang, I can't fight freely if I have to protect you." General Song was assuming all along and wanted to watch the fight. He insisted on going and eventually the stranger had no alternative but to take him along.

Approaching the spot, Big Iron-hammer sent General Song up to an empty castle and said, "Just watch. Be careful not to make any sound, otherwise the robbers will discover you." At this moment the cock crowed and the moon sank down. Stars shone out over the wilderness, so that figures a hundred paces away could be seen.

The stranger sped downwards, blowing his horn a couple of times. All at once more than two dozen cavalrymen from every direction gathered. Besides there were more than a hundred foot bandits with bows as well. A robber rode towards the stranger

231

曰：“奈何殺吾兄？”言未畢，客呼曰：“椎！”賊應聲落馬，人馬盡裂。眾賊環而進，客從容揮椎，人馬四面仆地下，殺三十許人。宋將軍屏息觀之，股慄欲墮。忽聞客大呼曰：“吾去矣！”但見地塵起，黑煙滾滾，東向馳去，後遂不復至。

魏禧《魏叔子文集》

with his sabre and roared out: "Why did you kill my brother?" Hardly had his words been spoken when the stranger shouted, "Watch out!" The robber fell off the horse at the shout, and both he and his horse were smashed. The gang of robbers then surrounded the stranger and began attacking him. He wielded his hammer easily in defence, and the robbers and their horses fell to the ground in all directions. Three dozen robbers were killed. General Song watched with bated breath, his legs trembling. He could hardly hold himself. Suddenly he heard the stranger yell, "I'm going!" At the same time with clouds of dust set flying and dark smoke billowing, the stranger sped towards the east and never returned.

Wei Xi (1624-1680)
Wei Shu Zi Wen Ji (Collected Works of Wei Shu Zi)

93. 何惜一官

　　胡勵齋[1]以詞臣備兵常鎮。時鎮多點盜，每擒治一人，輒株連百餘家，捕吏按籍鉤索。胡毅然爭曰：鼠輩特欲緩須臾死，害及無辜，庸可信乎？使者數至，數不與，復正色曰：殺人媚人，我不為也；何惜一官，為數百人請命耶？卒力白之。

王晫《今世說》

---

(1) 胡亶，號勵齋。

93. Don't Mind Losing My Position

Once Hu Lizhai was a civil official in command of the garrisons in Changzhou and Zhenjiang. At that time many cunning bandits haunted Zhenjiang. Whenever a bandit was arrested, the posse would search for people according to the household register, and hundreds of families would be involved in the case. Hu argued against the cops strongly: "Since the shabby bandits fear instant execution, they often frame up the innocent. How can you believe them?"

Runners from the central government came to Hu again and again, ordering him to send up the arrested people, but each time Hu refused. He said firmly, "I can't kill people for the purpose of flattering someone. I don't mind losing my position if I could help and save hundreds of people!" He proved their innocence at last.

Wang Zhuo
Jin Shi Shuo (Contemporary Accounts of Old Episodes)

94. 鳥語

　　中州[1]境有道士，募食鄉村。食已，聞鸚鳴，因告主人使慎火。問故，答曰：“鳥云：‘大火難救，可怕！’”眾笑之，竟不備。明日，果火，延燒數家，始驚其神。好事者追及之，稱為仙。道士曰：“我不過知鳥語耳，何仙也！”適有皂花雀鳴樹上，眾問何語。曰：“雀言：‘初六養之，初六養之；十四、十六殤之。’想此家雙生矣。今日為初十，不出五六日，當俱死也。”詢之，果生二子；無何，並死，其日悉符。邑令聞其奇，招之，延為客。時羣鴨過，因問之，對曰：“明公內室，必相爭也。鴨云：‘罷罷！偏向他！偏向他！’”令大服，蓋妻妾反脣，令適被喧聒而出也。因留居署中，優禮之。時辨鳥言，多奇中。而道士樸野，

---

(1) 中州：今河南省境。

236

94. What the Birds Say

There was a Taoist priest from Henan Province, who used to go begging for alms from village to village. Once after he had finished eating, he heard the orioles singing. On listening to them, he said to everybody around that they should all watch out for fire. When asked why, he replied that he heard the birds saying, "A big fire inextinguishable, terrible!" The people scoffed at it and took no precaution.

The next day a fire did break out and destroyed a number of houses. Only then were the people alerted. Some were curious to follow him around, calling him *xian* (a Taoist deity). He replied: "I am not an immortal, only I can understand the speech of birds." As there were some sparrows singing in a tree, those following him asked him what the birds were saying. He replied, "The birds said, 'Born on the sixth, born on the sixth, but dead on the fourteenth and the sixteenth.' This means that a family here had born twins. Today is the tenth, and in five or six days both will die." They went off after this to look for a family that had born twins. Sure enough they found the twins who later died as was described by the sparrows.

The local magistrate heard of this, and invited the priest to be his guest at home. At the time of their meeting there was a flock of ducks waddling past, and the magistrate asked the priest what the ducks were saying. He replied, "I suspect that Your Honour must have been having a domestic dispute as they say, 'Stop, stop! Side with her! Side with her!'" The magistrate was convinced as his wife and his concubine were having a quarrel and he had to leave the house to shun the noise. He decided to retain the priest as a guest and treated him generously. The priest often interpreted the words of the birds for him which mostly turned out to be correct, but often in a rude and outright manner.

肆言輒無所忌。令最貪，一切供用諸物，皆折為錢以入之。一日，方坐，羣鴨復來，令又詰之。答曰：“今日所言，不與前同，乃為明公會計耳。”問：“何計？”曰：“彼云：‘蠟燭一百八，銀朱一千八。’”令慚，疑其相譏。道士求去，令不許。踰數日，宴客，忽聞杜宇。客問之。答曰：“鳥云：‘丟官去。’”眾愕然失色。令大怒，立逐而出。未幾，令果以墨敗。嗚乎！此仙人儆戒之，而惜乎危厲熏心者，不之悟也。

蒲松齡《聊齋志異》

It happened that the magistrate was greedy. He lined his own pockets by selling for money all the articles for public use. One day the ducks passed by and he asked what they said. The priest replied: "What they say today is different from before. They settle an account with Your Honour." "What account?" asked the magistrate, and the priest replied: "One hundred and eighty gold coins for candles, and one thousand eight hundred for vermilion." The magistrate was ashamed when he heard this, and he suspected the priest of making a joke of him. Shortly after this the priest wished to leave, but he would not allow it.

A few days later the magistrate was throwing a party for friends of his when a cuckoo was heard. Somebody asked what the bird was saying and the priest replied: "Dismissed from the service." Those present were surprised while the magistrate was infuriated. He had the priest dragged out of the premises.

Not long after this the magistrate was dismissed from his position. Even if *xian* had given the warning he would not have listened, as he was already blinded with greed.

Pu Songling (1630-1715)
Liao Zhai Zhi Yi (Records about Oddities in Liao Zhai)

95. 鸚鵡

　　關中[1]商人，得能言鸚鵡於隴山，愛而食之甚勤。偶事下獄，歸時歎恨不已。鸚鵡曰：“郎在獄數日已不堪，鸚鵡遭閉累年，奈何？”商感而放之。後商同輩有過隴山者，鸚鵡必於林間問曰：“郎無恙否？幸寄聲，幸寄聲。”

王言《聖師錄》

---

(1)關中：相當於今陝西省境中部。

95. A Parrot

A trader from Guanzhong obtained a talking parrot in the Long
Mountains. He was very fond of it and often fed it by hand. Once
the man was thrown into prison for a few days. After he was released, he still felt nasty about the affair. The parrot said, "You
were in prison for merely a couple of days and it is already so
unbearable to you; your parrot has been in a cage for years, how
would you feel about that?" The man was touched and released
the bird.

After that, whenever associates of that trader passed through
the Long Mountains, the parrot living in the forest would ask
them, "How is the gentleman? Please send him my regards, please
send him my regards."

Wang Yan
Sheng Shi Lu (Records of Sages)

96. 鶴

　　陳州倅盧某，蓄二鶴，甚馴。一創死，一哀鳴不
食。盧勉飼之，乃就食。一旦鳴繞盧側。盧曰："爾欲
去，不爾羈也。"鶴振翮雲際，數四徊翔乃去。盧老病
無子。後三年，歸臥黃蒲溪上。晚秋蕭索，曳杖林間，
忽有一鶴盤空，鳴聲淒斷。盧仰祝曰："若非我陳州侶
耶？果爾，即當下。"鶴竟投入懷中。以喙牽衣，旋舞
不釋。遂引之歸。後盧歿，鶴亦不食死，家人瘞之墓
左。

　　　　　　　　　　　　　　　　　王言《聖師錄》

96. A Crane

Governor Lu of Chenzhou raised two cranes. Both were very tame. One day, when one of the cranes died the other wailed plaintively and refused any food. Lu had to force it to eat. Another day, the crane was crowing beside Lu, and Lu said, "If you wish to leave, I will not stop you." The crane fluttered its wings and soared up, and after wheeling about in the sky for a while, it flew away.

When Lu was old, he was overcome by illness, and he had no son. He spent his last three years in Huang Pu Xi. One bleak autumn day he took a walk with a stick in the woods. Suddenly a crane hovered over him, crowing sadly. Lu looked up and uttered, "Aren't you my friend from Chenzhou? If so, you should come down." The crane landed and leaned against his bosom. It then pulled his clothes with its beak and hopped around without pause. Lu led it home.

Later when Lu passed away, the crane wouldn't eat any longer, and before long it died too. The family of Lu buried the crane beside Lu's grave.

Wang Yan
Sheng Shi Lu (Records of Sages)

97. 偷畫

　　有白日入人家偷畫者，方卷出門，主人自外歸。賊
窘，持畫而跪，曰：「此小人家外祖像也。窮極無奈，
願以易米數斗。」主人大笑，嗤其愚妄，揮叱之去，竟
不取視。登堂，則所懸趙子昂[1]畫失矣。

袁枚《新齊諧》

---

(1) 趙子昂：名孟頫（1254-1355），元代大書畫家。

97. The Theft of a Painting

Once a man broke into a house to steal a painting in broad daylight. As he rolled up the scroll and was hurrying out, the owner returned. The thief, feeling desperate, knelt down and held up the painting, pleading: "This is a portrait of my maternal grandfather. As I am stricken with poverty, I wish to exchange it for some rice."

The householder burst out laughing, sneering at his absurd behaviour, and waved him out without even thinking about the picture. However when he reached the hall, he discovered the painting by the famous painter, Zhao Zi'ang, was missing.

Yuan Mei (1716-1797)
Xin Qi Xie (New Humour from Qi)

98. 唐打獵

　　族兄中涵知旌德縣時，近城有虎，暴傷獵戶數人，不能捕。邑人請曰："非聘徽州唐打獵，不能除此患也！"（休寧戴東原曰：明代有唐某，甫新婚而戕於虎。其婦後生一子，祝之曰："爾不能殺虎，非我子也！後世子孫如不能殺虎，亦皆非我子孫！"故唐世世能捕虎。）乃遣吏持幣往。歸報：唐氏選藝至精者二人，行且至。至，則一老翁，鬚髮皓然，時咯咯作嗽；一童子，十六七耳。大失望。姑令具食。老翁察中涵意不滿，半跪啟曰："聞此虎距城不五里，先往捕之，賜食未晚也。"遂命役導往。役至谷口，不敢行。老翁哂

246

98. Tang the Hunter

My cousin, Zhong Han, was once magistrate of the Jingde County. At that time, a tiger had killed several hunters in the neighbourhood, and nobody had managed to catch it. The people called on the magistrate to employ the services of Tang the Hunter to catch the tiger, feeling that no other person was equal to the task.

According to Dai Dongyuan of Xiuning, the story was that in the Ming Dynasty, a hunter called Tang was killed by a tiger soon after he had got married. His wife was pregnant and later gave birth to a son. She prayed and made a wish about her son: "If you can't kill tigers, you won't be my son any longer, and any of your sons and grandsons who fail at this may not consider themselves to be my descendants." Owing to this all of the Tang men were expert at killing tigers.

Zhong Han despatched men to call on the Tang hunters, entrusting a large sum of money to them for this purpose.

On their return, these men stated that they had employed the best of the Tang men and that they would arrive in no time. When they arrived, one was an old man with a white beard and white hair, who coughed and wheezed every now and then, the other was a sixteen-year-old lad. The magistrate was greatly disappointed at their appearance. However, he ordered to treat them to food first. Noticing that the magistrate seemed disappointed the old man knelt on one knee and said, "I hear that this tiger is only five *li*[1] from the town, so we had better go and catch it before we eat." The magistrate ordered his men to guide them, and so they set out.

Arriving at the mouth of a ravine, the men would go no further.

_____

(1) 1 *li* =1/2 km

曰：「我在，爾尚畏耶？」入谷將半，老翁顧童子曰：
「此畜似尚睡，汝呼之醒。」童子作虎嘯聲。果自林中
出，徑搏老翁，老翁手一短斧，縱八九寸，橫半之，奮
臂屹立。虎撲至，側首讓之。虎自頂上躍過，已血流仆
地。視之，自領下至尾閭，皆觸斧裂矣！乃厚贈遣之。
老翁自言練臂十年，練目十年。其目以毛帚掃之不瞬；
其臂使壯夫攀之，懸身下縋不能動。莊子曰：「習伏
眾，神巧者不過習者之門。」信夫！嘗見史舍人嗣彪，
暗中捉筆書條幅，與秉燭無異；又聞靜海勵文恪公[1]，
剪方寸紙一百片，書一字其上，片片向日疊映，無一筆
絲毫出入。均習之而已矣，非別有謬巧也。

　　　　　　　　　　　　　　　紀昀《閱微草堂筆記》

---

(1) 勵文恪公：勵杜訥，諡文恪。

248

But the old man smiled: "With me here, how come you are still scared?" When they had half entered the ravine, he glanced back at the boy and said, "This tiger seems to be asleep, go and wake it up!" The boy then roared like a tiger, and in no time the tiger rushed out at them from among the trees and leapt at the old man. The old man stood his ground, raising a short axe, eight *cun*[2] long and four wide. As the tiger was about to crush him, he parried to one side, and the tiger jumped over him, landing on the ground with blood streaming out. The men crowded around and discovered that the tiger was neatly cut right from the chin to the tip of its tail as it touched the axe. The magistrate then generously rewarded the Tangs for their help.

The old man recounted that he had trained his arms and eyes for ten years. He could stare without blinking even when his eyes were brushed with a feather duster and his arms were so strong that even a strong man could not move them a little.

Zhuang Zi, the famous ancient Chinese philosopher, said, "The achievements through practice are always convincing. A person who is born clever can never surpass one who constantly practises." This is most certainly true. An official called Shi Sibiao could write in darkness just as well as he could in candle light. I also heard of His Excellency Li Wenke (1628-1703) of Jing Hai, who had a hundred pieces of paper and wrote a character on each. Placed on top of one another and held against the light the hundred characters were seen to overlap precisely to form one character. This is due only to practice, and not to magic.

Ji Yun (1724-1805)
Yue Wei Cao Tang Bi Ji (Notes Written in Yue Wei Cottage)

---

(2) 1 *cun*=3.3cm

99. 避諛

　　有舊家子夜行深山中，迷不得路。望一岩洞，聊投憩息，則前輩某公在焉。懼不敢進。然某公招邀甚切。度無他害，姑前拜謁。寒溫勞苦如平生。略問家事，共相悲慨。因問："公佳城在某所，何獨游至此？"某公喟然曰："我在世無過失。然讀書第隨人作計，做官第循分供職，亦無所樹立。不意葬數年後，墓前忽見一巨碑。螭額篆文，是我官階姓字。碑文所述，則我皆不知。其中略有影響者，又都過實。我一生樸拙，意已不安，加以游人過讀，時有譏評，鬼物聚觀，更多訕笑。我不耐其聒，因避居於此。惟歲時祭掃，到彼一視子孫耳。"士人曲相寬慰曰："仁人孝子，非此不足以榮親。蔡中郎(1)不免愧詞，韓吏部(2)亦嘗諛墓。古多此例，公亦何必介懷？"某公正色曰："是非之公，人心

---

(1) 蔡中郎：東漢蔡邕，董卓時官中郎將。
(2) 韓吏部：唐韓愈，穆宗時任吏部侍郎。

250

99. To Shun the Flatteries

Once a descendant of a prominent family, while travelling deep in the mountains at night, lost his way. As he saw a cave, he intended to have a rest in it. To his astonishment, a late senior of his family was there in the cave. He was too frightened to go forth. However the old gentleman invited him enthusiastically. Supposing it would mean no harm, the descendant went forward to greet him. They exchanged a few words of regards as if they had known each other. The elder asked about the family, then they both sighed.

"Where is your esteemed grave? Why did you come here?" asked the descendant.

The elder sighed, "When I was in the world, I committed no mistake. However I studied as others did, officiated law-abidingly and didn't make any great achievements either. But a few years after my burial, a huge tombstone was erected by my grave unexpectedly. Carved with dragons, the tablet had my name and offices written on it in seal characters. What the inscriptions say is totally beyond my knowledge. Some stories were true, but exaggerated. Since I was always honest in my life, the inflated epitaph upset me. Moreover, many tourists read the epitaph while passing by, and made sarcastic comments. A lot of ghosts gathered round my grave to have a look, and they poured pungent ridicule on me. I couldn't put up with their gossips, so I fled here to live in seclusion. Only on the days of memorial ceremonies do I return to my grave in order to see my descendants."

The descendant comforted him tactfully: "Your dutiful sons thought it was the only way to glorify their parent. Even Cai Yong (133-192) failed to refrain from inflated words, and Han Yu (768-824) flattered his late seniors as well. There are many such instances in history, why should you feel uneasy?" The elder said

俱在。人即可誑，自問己慚。況公論俱在，誑亦何益！榮親當在顯揚，何必以虛詞招謗乎？不謂後起勝流，所見皆如是也！」拂衣竟起。士人惘惘而歸。

紀昀《閱微草堂筆記》

firmly, "Anyone can judge between truth and falsehood. I'm embarrassed when others create stories about me. Moreover, there's still justice in the world, what's the good of deceptive stories? The right way to glorify parents is by accomplishment, why should they create deception and ask for slander? Even you, a promising young man, should think like them!" No sooner had he finished speaking than he got up with disappointment. The descendant left in disconsolation.

Ji Yun (1724-1805)
Yue Wei Cao Tang Bi Ji (Notes Written in Yue Wei Cottage)

100. 滿朝皆忠臣

　　高宗循衛河南巡，舟行倚窗，見道旁農夫耕作，為
向所未見，輒顧而樂之。至山左[(1)]某邑，欲悉民間疾
苦，因召一農夫至御舟，問歲穫之豐歉，農業之大略，
地方長官之賢否。農夫奏對，頗愜聖意。尋又令遍視隨
扈諸臣，兼詢姓氏。群臣以農夫奉旨詢問，於上前不敢
不以名對，中多有恐農夫採輿論上聞致觸聖怒者，皆股
栗失常。農夫閱竟，奏曰：“滿朝皆忠臣。”上問何以
知之。農夫奏稱：“吾見演劇時，淨腳所扮之奸臣，如
曹操、秦檜，皆面塗白粉如雪，今諸大臣無作此狀者，
故知其皆忠臣也。”上大噱。

徐珂：《清稗類鈔》

---

(1) 山左：山東省的別稱，因其地在太行山的左側。

100.   All of Them Are Loyal

Emperor Gao Zong (1711-1799) of the Qing Dynasty took an inspection tour southwards by royal barge along the Wei River. By the window he enjoyed the view of peasants working in the fields, which he had never seen before. On arriving in a county of the Shandong Province, he called a peasant to his ship in order to figure out the weal and woe of the people. He inquired of him about the year's harvest, farm work and the conduct of local officials. The answers from the farmer quite satisfied him.

Then the Emperor had the peasant look at his attendant officials around and ask their names. The officials thinking that the peasant was under His Majesty's order, dared not conceal their real names before the Emperor. Being afraid that the peasant would report the public opinion which would drive the Emperor angry, some officials shook tremendously. After reading their faces, the peasant said to the Emperor, "All of them are loyal." His Majesty asked how he knew it and the reply was, "I saw on the stage the actors in the roles of the treacherous court officials like Cao Cao and Qin Gui put snow-white make-up on their faces. Now since none of your attendant officials appears like that, I can tell that all of them are loyal."

The Emperor burst into laughter.

Xu Ke
Qing Bei Lei Chao (Classified Anecdotes of the Qing Dynasty)

中國歷代極短篇一百則＝100 ancient Chinese
miniature stories／馬家駒編譯. -- 臺灣初
版. -- 臺北市：臺灣商務，1995[民84]
　　面；　公分. --（一百叢書；16）
　　ISBN 957-05-1122-2（平裝）

857　　　　　　　　　　　　　　84002608

一百叢書⑯

100 ANCIENT CHINESE MINIATURE STORIES

中國歷代極短篇一百則

定價新臺幣 280 元

編　譯　者　馬　家　駒
叢 書 編 輯　羅　　　斯
執 行 編 輯　金　　　堅

出　版　者
印　刷　所　臺灣商務印書館股份有限公司
　　　　　　臺北市 10036 重慶南路 1 段 37 號
　　　　　　電話：(02)23116118 ・ 23115538
　　　　　　傳眞：(02)23710274 ・ 23701091
　　　　　　讀者服務專線：0800-056196
　　　　　　E-mail：cptw@ms12.hinet.net
　　　　　　郵政劃撥：0000165 － 1 號
　　　　　　出版事業
　　　　　　登 記 證：局版北市業字第 993 號

・1994 年 11 月香港初版
・1995 年 5 月臺灣初版第一次印刷
・2001 年 8 月臺灣初版第二次印刷
本書經商務印書館（香港）股份有限公司授權出版
（原書名：中國歷代微型小說一百篇）

ISBN 957-05-1122-2(平裝)　　　　　b 56724040

一百叢書　　100 SERIES

英漢　·　漢英對照

1 世界著名寓言一百篇 ....陳德運 / 李仲 / 周國珍譯
100 World's Great Fables

2 名人演說一百篇.............................石幼珊譯 / 張隆溪校
100 Famous Speeches

3 名人書信一百封................................ ....黃繼忠譯
100 World's Great Letters

4 聖經故事一百篇...................劉意青 / 馮國忠 / 白曉冬譯
100 Bible Stories /

5 希臘羅馬神話一百篇.................................陶潔等選譯
100 Myths of Greece and Rome

6 唐詩一百首..................張廷琛 / Bruce M.Wilson 選譯
100 Tang Poems

7 莎劇精選一百段...黃兆傑編譯
100 Passages from the Dramatic Writings of Shakespeare

8 中國神話及志怪小說一百篇........................丁往道選譯
100 Chinese Myths and Fantasies

9 中國古代寓言一百篇.............................喬車潔玲選譯
100 Ancient Chinese Fables

10 中國成語故事一百篇................................楊立義選譯
100 Chinese Idioms and Their Stories

11 唐宋詞一百首..許淵沖選譯
100 Tang and Song Cipoems

12 中國歷代笑話一百篇................................盧允中選譯
100 Chinese Jokes through the Ages

13 現代英美詩一百首....................................張曼儀主編
100 Modern English Poems

14 莎士比亞十四行詩一百首............................屠岸編譯
100 Sonnets by Shakespeare

15 孫子兵法一百則..羅志野譯
Sun Tzu's the Art of War

16 中國歷代極短篇一百則............................馬家駒選譯
100 Ancient Chinese Miniature Stories

讀者回函卡

感謝您對本館的支持，為加強對您的服務，請填妥此卡，免付郵資寄回，可隨時收到本館最新出版訊息，及享受各種優惠。

姓名：＿＿＿＿＿＿＿＿＿＿＿＿＿＿ 性別：□男 □女

出生日期：＿＿年＿＿月＿＿日

職業：□學生 □公務（含軍警） □家管 □服務 □金融 □製造
　　　□資訊 □大眾傳播 □自由業 □農漁牧 □退休 □其他

學歷：□高中以下（含高中） □大專 □研究所（含以上）

地址：＿＿＿＿＿＿＿＿＿＿＿＿＿＿＿＿＿＿＿＿＿＿＿＿
　　　＿＿＿＿＿＿＿＿＿＿＿＿＿＿＿＿＿＿＿＿＿＿＿＿

電話：（H）＿＿＿＿＿＿＿＿＿（O）＿＿＿＿＿＿＿＿＿

購買書名：＿＿＿＿＿＿＿＿＿＿＿＿＿＿＿＿＿＿＿＿＿＿

您從何處得知本書？

　　　□書店 □報紙廣告 □報紙專欄 □雜誌廣告 □DM廣告
　　　□傳單 □親友介紹 □電視廣播 □其他

您對本書的意見？（A/滿意 B/尚可 C/需改進）

　　　內容＿＿＿＿ 編輯＿＿＿＿ 校對＿＿＿＿ 翻譯＿＿＿＿
　　　封面設計＿＿＿＿ 價格＿＿＿＿ 其他＿＿＿＿＿＿＿＿

您的建議：＿＿＿＿＿＿＿＿＿＿＿＿＿＿＿＿＿＿＿＿＿＿
　　　　　＿＿＿＿＿＿＿＿＿＿＿＿＿＿＿＿＿＿＿＿＿＿
　　　　　＿＿＿＿＿＿＿＿＿＿＿＿＿＿＿＿＿＿＿＿＿＿

臺灣商務印書館

台北市重慶南路一段三十七號　電話：（02）23116118・23115538
讀者服務專線：080056196　傳真：（02）23710274
郵撥：0000165-1號　E-mail：cptw@ms12.hinet.net

100臺北市重慶南路一段37號

臺灣商務印書館　收

對摺寄回，謝謝！

傳統現代　並翼而翔

Flying with the wings of tradition and modernity.